Samuel French Acting Edition

Wrong Turn at Lungfish

by Garry Marshall
& Lowell Ganz

SAMUEL FRENCH

SAMUELFRENCH.COM   SAMUELFRENCH.CO.UK

ISBN 978-0-573-69482-0

www.SamuelFrench.com
www.SamuelFrench.co.uk

FOR PRODUCTION ENQUIRIES

UNITED STATES AND CANADA

Info@SamuelFrench.com

1-866-598-8449

UNITED KINGDOM AND EUROPE

Plays@SamuelFrench.co.uk

020-7255-4302

Each title is subject to availability from Samuel French, depending upon country of performance. Please be aware that *WRONG TURN AT LUNGFISH* may not be licensed by Samuel French in your territory. Professional and amateur producers should contact the nearest Samuel French office or licensing partner to verify availability.

Wrong Turn at Lungfish had its world premiere at the Steppenwolf Theatre on June 6, 1990, Randall Arney, Artistic Director, Stephen B. Eich, Managing Director.

Wrong Turn at Lungfish opened at the Promenade Theatre in New York City, in February, 1993 with the following cast (in order of appearance):

PETER RAVENSWAAL---------------George C. Scott

NURSE ---------------------------------Kelli Williams

ANITA MERENDINO ---------------------- Jami Gertz

DOMINIC DE CAESAR-------------------Tony Danza

Directed by: Garry Marshall
Set Design by: David Jenkins
Costumes by: Erin Quigley
Lighting by: Peter Kaczorowski
Sound by: Tom Morse
Casting by: Lynn Stalmaster

CHARACTERS

PETER RAVENSWAAL – Early to late 60's. Virile, strong, gruff-voiced and cynical. Other than being blind, you'd never guess he's ill.

NURSE – Complaining, immature young girl who is somehow going to be a good nurse, some day.

ANITA MERENDINO – Mid-to-late 20's, early 30's, tough street girl. Very optimistic and cheerful in order to hide a low self-esteem.

DOMINIC DE CAESAR – Anita's boyfriend. Late 20's, early 30's. A good-looking, funny, charming but not brilliant street guy who can turn mean suddenly.

TIME & PLACE

The Present.
A hospital room somewhere in New York City.

ACT I

Scene 1	Noon
Scene 2	Another day – noon
Scene 3	Another day – evening

Intermission

ACT II

Scene 1	The next day – mid-morning
Scene 2	Several hours later

Wrong Turn At Lungfish

ACT I

SCENE. The time is the present and we see a single room on the third floor of a New York City hospital.

We hear BEETHOVEN'S NINTH SYMPHONY playing As LIGHTS come full up the music goes out It's around lunchtime, but there's a little sunshine coming through the room's lone window There's not much of anything in this room No flowers, no gift boxes of candy, no get well cards taped to the wall There's one hospital bed with a night table on either side of it On one night table is a pile of books, a radio-cassette player, and some audio tapes There are two doors, one leading out to the corridor, the other to a small bathroom in the room Next to the bed is a straight-back chair, and on the opposite wall is a TV set with two chairs under it There's a hook to hang coats behind night table nearest corridor door The room is empty and the door out to the corridor is open For a moment there is silence The quiet is broken by offstage SHOUTING

NURSE *(Offstage)* Mr Ravenswaal. Mr. Ravenswaal! Come back here!

RAVENSWAAL. *(Offstage)* Leave me alone!

NURSE *(Offstage.)* Mr Ravenswaal, come back—look out!

(HE bangs into something else There's a CRASH)

RAVENSWAAL. *(Offstage)* What was that?!
NURSE. *(Offstage)* That was everybody's lunch.
RAVENSWAAL. *(Offstage.)* Well, then help me!
NURSE. *(Offstage)* All right! Here. This way. I have
to clean up this mess you made.

*(PETER RAVENSWAAL careens into the room alone. He
is in his early sixties HE wears dark glasses, a robe
over his pajamas and carries a cane which HE swings
dangerously Using the cane ineffectively, HE stumbles,
grabbing his bed for safety HE takes off his robe and
throws robe, glasses and cane on the floor The NURSE
is still out in the hall cleaning RAVENSWAAL holds
his head, obviously in pain, and worried, for a beat
Then the NURSE enters the room and his entire attitude
changes to a peppier but grouchy patient The NURSE
is a young girl in her early twenties who gives the
impression that nothing ever goes smoothly for her)*

NURSE. *(Offstage.)* Thanks, Raul. *(Enters, begging)*
Mr. Ravenswaal. I have to walk you. Why did you run
away?
RAVENSWAAL I have to use the bathroom. Help me.
(HE gets off of bed and sticks out his hand)
NURSE. You're supposed to try to get around by
yourself.
RAVENSWAAL. I tried. I failed. Help me!
NURSE Dr. Wells gave strict orders.

RAVENSWAAL. Dr. Wells ... In an enlightened society, that man would be killed and his body put on public display—Ow! (*During the preceding, HE heads for the bathroom, but does not see the tray table which is in his way, HE bangs into it.*) Damn it help me before I break my neck!

NURSE. (*Frustrated.*) I was told not to!

RAVENSWAAL. (*New attitude.*) You're right. I completely understand. I'll go right here. (*HE pulls out the night table drawer and makes believe he's going to urinate in it.*)

NURSE. (*Rushing to him*) All right! All right. Come on. I'll take you. But don't tell Dr. Wells. (*SHE takes his arm and leads him to the bathroom.*) Do you want to meet the people from the blind institute? *They'll* show you how to use your cane. They have—

RAVENSWAAL. (*Offstage.*) No. (*Enters bathroom*) Wait for me.

NURSE You're six steps away—

RAVENSWAAL. Wait for me!

(*SHE closes the door, then pantomimes machine-gunning the bathroom door SHE seems like a kid The corridor door opens and ANITA enters ANITA is in her late twenties with an innocent-looking face and a guilty-looking body SHE's carrying a large paper bag, a purse, and a coat SHE's in a nice mood. SHE catches the nurse "machine-gunning"*)

ANITA. Hi.

NURSE. (*Startled*) Oh Hi! Uh ... I was just ... You came to see him?

ANITA.Yes.

NURSE. Visiting hours aren't until two p.m. Two to three p.m. ...

ANITA. (*Puts her stuff down and hands the NURSE a note.*) They gave me this.

NURSE. (*Reads and is satisfied she's okay.*) Oh. (*Then.*) You really like hanging around with these old people?

ANITA. Yes. I learn things from them. They got a lot of wisdom.

NURSE They got a lot of complaints! He's in the bathroom. Would you put him back into bed for me? It's a piss storm in here today. One nurse is out sick ... And two are testifying at malpractice suits....

ANITA. Sure I'll help him. I'm very good with the patients. How long has he been blind?

NURSE. I don't know—a couple months—and usually by *now* they try to do something by themselves. Not him.

ANITA. How come?

NURSE. I'm a nurse, not a psychiatrist and I'm done ... tell him lunch is going to be late because he knocked over the food cart ... you hear the crash? He woke up two patients from comas

(*The NURSE exits ANITA looks around. SHE examines a couple of his books The TOILET flushes, and RAVENSWAAL comes out of the bathroom*)

RAVENSWAAL I'm finished Another demonstration of what the handicapped can accomplish if they're given half a chance. Help me!

ANITA (*Goes and takes his hand*) Here we go.

RAVENSWAAL. *(Freezes.)* That's not you.

ANITA. No, it's me.

RAVENSWAAL. Where is she?

ANITA. You mean her?

RAVENSWAAL. Yes. Who are you?

ANITA. It's me.

RAVENSWAAL. *(Frustrated.)* It's a carnival of pronouns.

ANITA. What?

RAVENSWAAL. I don't know. Third base. Who are you?

ANITA. Oh! I'm your reader, Anita. I was here last week. Mr. Ravenswaal. *(SHE helps him into bed.)*

RAVENSWAAL. Anita? Nasal Anita?

ANITA. *(Good natured.)* That's me.

RAVENSWAAL. Anita, I'm sure you're very sweet. And for a young girl to volunteer her time reading to blind people could be considered admirable.

ANITA. Thank you. It's no biggie, the bus lets me off right at the corner.

RAVENSWAAL. But the fact is I've called and asked for a different reader.

ANITA. Oh, I know. They told me you didn't want me. But no one else will come to you no more.

RAVENSWAAL. Any more.

ANITA. No one else will come to you any more.

RAVENSWAAL. *(Mad.)* They can all go to hell.

ANITA. You know they have books on tape. Whole books on tape. Whole books read by stars of stage, screen, and television.

RAVENSWAAL. No, no. I'm afraid I can't abide Keats being read to me by Ed McMahon.

ANITA. Well, I'm what's left. (*Cheerful.*) Should I start reading something? I bought the books. (*SHE gets her paper bag*)

RAVENSWAAL. Why did you come back? Didn't I throw pudding at you?

ANITA. Yeah, you missed.

RAVENSWAAL. Of course I missed. I'm blind. So why did you come back?

ANITA. I don't know. I guess I never met a college principal before.

RAVENSWAAL (*Correcting*) Dean.

ANITA. Anita.

RAVENSWAAL. What?

ANITA. Me.

RAVENSWAAL. Go back, go back! You said "principal." I said "dean."

ANITA. (*Firmly*) Anita.

RAVENSWAAL. Stop that!

ANITA. (*Yells.*) Is your first name Dean or not?

RAVENSWAAL. No. My name is Peter. I was the dean of a college.

ANITA. Ohh ...

RAVENSWAAL. That's why you came back?

ANITA. Yeah. I never met a dean before.

RAVENSWAAL. No doubt. I could tell that from the way you read.

ANITA. (*Agrees*) Yeah.

RAVENSWAAL. I just insulted you.

ANITA. (*Cheerful*) I know. You insult everybody. Kills me. So how are you? Did you see the doctor today?

RAVENSWAAL. Yes, I consulted all three of those ... geniuses.

ANITA. What did they say?

RAVENSWAAL. That's none of your business. (*Curtly.*) You'd better go.

ANITA. Okay. I was just chatting. The nurses say you don't get no visitors.

RAVENSWAAL. Any visitors.

ANITA. Yeah. I feel sorry for you. I take an interest in all my patients.

RAVENSWAAL. You **don't have** any patients. You're a girl who comes on her lunch hour and reads to any poor slob who can't see.

ANITA. Yeah. I like to say "my patients." It makes me feel more important. You know like I'm *doing* something. It gives me ...

RAVENSWAAL. (*Interrupts.*) Some sense of purpose in your otherwise trivial existence.

ANITA. (*Glad he got it SHE puts bag in drawer.*) Yeah! You figured me out.

RAVENSWAAL. But why did you choose to do *this*?

ANITA. Why? (*Enthusiastic*) That's an interesting story ...

RAVENSWAAL. An interesting *short* story?

ANITA. Yeah, short. My grandmother was blind. So when I was a little girl I read to her, the magazines. *Soap Opera Digest* She liked to know everybody's business. Then she was in a home with *other* blind people, so I started reading to the other blind people ...

RAVENSWAAL. How long was your grandmother blind?

ANITA. The last ten years of her life.

RAVENSWAAL. (*Quietly.*) Not the best ten.

ANITA. (*Kindly.*) Must be hard to get used to, huh?

(SHE touches his arm gently but HE pulls his arm away abruptly.)

RAVENSWAAL. *(A beat)* What books did you bring?

ANITA. What you had me write on the list. The one by Schopenhauer. *(Pronounces "Schop" to rhyme with "hop")*

RAVENSWAAL. Schopenhauer.

ANITA. *(Corrects.)* Schopenhauer. John Keats, "The Poems." And I couldn't find the baseball book.

RAVENSWAAL. Baseball book?

ANITA. Yeah. The one by Casey Stengel. "Reds and the Blacks."

RAVENSWAAL. *(Bewildered)* Casey Stengel ... *(Realizing)* That's Stendahl! French novelist. 19th Century. Stendahl! *(Enraged)* Where's the pudding? *(HE gropes around for pudding)*

ANITA There's no pudding!

RAVENSWAAL. Go, goodbye. Go. Please go. *(HE turns on cassette player We hear BEETHOVEN'S NINTH.)*

ANITA. *(Crosses to purse and coat on hook)* Okay. I'll see you next week. Here's your change from the books. Oh, I got that other book too.

RAVENSWAAL. What other book?

(SHE puts change, one dollar and coins, in his drawer and pulls the "other" book, which is a small paperback, out of her purse)

ANITA. *A Hooker By Choice (Reads.)* "The story of a college girl who graduated erotica cum laude." *(SHE says "loud" for laude, then adds the "ee" sound)*

RAVENSWAAL. I know what it's about. You bought that book?

ANITA. You told me to.

RAVENSWAAL. (*A beat.*) Sit down. (*HE turns off cassette player Surprised*) You bought that book?

ANITA You asked me to.

RAVENSWAAL. I was being facetious.

ANITA Is that like horny?

RAVENSWAAL. No, that's like facetious.

ANITA. I was kinda surprised a dean would like this.

RAVENSWAAL. Read. I'm sure you'll have no trouble with these words.

(*SHE opens the book as HE takes the cassette out of the player*)

ANITA. There's no pictures. You're not missing anything. (*SHE gives him a playful poke*)

RAVENSWAAL. Don't poke. Read.

ANITA. (*Reads.*) "Chapter one. Cathy liked kicks " Well they get right into it, don't they? "Ever since the day she snuck into the football team's shower room and saw them soaping up their muscular firm bodies Then the water ran down and revealed their young manhood, glistening in the fluorescent shower lights as if to say, 'I'm a boy no longer.' "...

RAVENSWAAL. (*A long beat, then*) What happened? Did I go deaf too?

ANITA I'm sorry. I can't read this stuff.

RAVENSWAAL. You're offended?

ANITA. No. I don't want to read about sex right now. How about a little Schopenhauer?

RAVENSWAAL. I'm not going to do anything. If I couldn't even hit you with the pudding, I'm hardly a sexual threat.

ANITA. I wasn't worried about you being a sexual threat, Mr. Ravenswaal. I just don't like to think about sex.

RAVENSWAAL. You don't like sex?

ANITA. I like it. It's just bad for me to think about it too much.

RAVENSWAAL. Are you homely?

ANITA. (*Insulted.*) No. It's ... it's personal.

RAVENSWAAL. Try one chapter. Then we'll move on to something else. I love the style of writing, it amuses me. Besides, I'm getting used to the nasal quality in your voice.

ANITA. Thank you. I'll try. (*Reads.*) "Cathy's first experience was with Homer, the school's burly janitor. Homer's small brain was more than compensated for by his..."

RAVENSWAAL. Beethoven was deaf.

ANITA. What ?

RAVENSWAAL. The music I was just playing ... Beethoven's Ninth Symphony ... He wrote it when he was deaf.

ANITA. Who did?

RAVENSWAAL. Beethoven!

ANITA. He was deaf?

RAVENSWAAL. Yes. It makes me wonder. How would a man—deaf—at the end of his life—a life dominated by depression—write anything so uplifting—so optimistic as the "Ode to Joy"?

ANITA. Yeah, it sounds pretty fishy.

RAVENSWAAL. No. It's not "fishy." I don't suspect him of some deception—read.

ANITA. Now, you got me thinking. He wrote nine symphonies and he was deaf. I couldn't write one. And I had the highest score in the eighth grade hearing test.

RAVENSWAAL. How fascinating ... then you must have heard me ask you to read.

ANITA. Sure. It's very interesting talking to you, though. I'm going to enjoy coming here, this is fun.

RAVENSWAAL. I'm dying.

ANITA. Huh?

RAVENSWAAL. It won't be that much fun. The same thing that made me blind is now going to make me dead.

ANITA. (*Shaken*) When did they tell you?—

RAVENSWAAL. This morning. Read.

ANITA. Isn't there anything—

RAVENSWAAL. Read!

ANITA. "Homer's small brain was more than compensated for by his" ...

(*LIGHTS slowly dim*)

Scene 2

It's around lunchtime of another day in Mr. Ravenswaal's room RAVENSWAAL stands on a chair under the hospital room TV The TV hangs from the ceiling across from the bed The TV is not turned on HE has his arms protectively around the TV The NURSE

*hangs up phone and is obviously having a disagreement
with Mr RAVENSWAAL*

NURSE. (*On phone.*) All right, I'll try. (*Hangs up
phone and crosses to Ravenswaal*) I am a nurse! I am in a
position of responsibility and you have to do as I say.
RAVENSWAAL. You are not a real nurse. You're a
student nurse. And if you *become* a real nurse I will lose a
five dollar bet with Doctor Wells.
NURSE. (*Surprised*) Dr. Wells bet on me. Wow.
RAVENSWAAL. Young lady ...
NURSE. What?
RAVENSWAAL. I have the same *rights* in this
hospital as Mr Santoni. Why should he receive better
treatment?
NURSE. Because he's nicer and everybody likes him
more.
RAVENSWAAL. (*Victorious.*) Ah! That's the very
essence of democracy. The protection of the disliked.
NURSE. Look. It's simple. Mr. Santoni watches a lot
of TV. His set flickers. You never turn yours on. So we're
switching yours with his. What's the problem?
RAVENSWAAL. You've given everything I own to
Mr. Santoni. You gave him my tray table, my hangers,
and my best chair. Next you'll be giving him my clothes!
I'll be damned if he gets my TV!
NURSE. I'll have Raul come in here when you're
sleeping and he'll yank it out.
RAVENSWAAL. I'll smash it first. Scorched earth
policy.
NURSE. Fine. But do you know why you have a
student nurse? Because the real nurses won't come to you

anymore. And if you stay up there much longer, I'll move your furniture around to different places!

(*SHE storms out and bumps into ANITA as she goes NURSE looks at him ANITA holds coffee cup*)

NURSE. Would you believe he won't give up his TV set and he can't even see? It's a zoo. Look at him!
ANITA. He looks pretty frisky today.
NURSE. Yeah, they've pumped him full of pills and he went climbing. See if you can get him down. (*To Ravenswaal*) I'm going down to the gift shop now to buy Mr. Santoni a present!

(*NURSE exits ANITA walks toward Ravenswaal SHE is amused*)

ANITA What are you doing up there, Mr. Ravenswaal?
RAVENSWAAL. I'm exercising my territorial imperative.
ANITA. Good. Whatever you said. Would you like to come down here with me?
RAVENSWAAL. Physically, yes. Intellectually, not without scuba gear.
ANITA (*Amused SHE takes his arm*) That was a shot at me wasn't it? (*SHE's helping him down*) I understand. If someone tried to take my TV I'd go crazy. What's your favorite show?
RAVENSWAAL. Off.
ANITA What?
RAVENSWAAL. I never watch.

ANITA. Oh, like my grandma. You just listen. She loved the game shows.

RAVENSWAAL. Did she?

ANITA. You should probably go on those shows. You'd be a whiz. And you're blind, that's very good. They like people with a gimmick.

RAVENSWAAL. (*Laughs*) I'll keep that in mind. Thank you.

ANITA. Ready for reading?

RAVENSWAAL. Yes ... (*Then.*) Anita, I hope my behavior the other day didn't upset you. I was a little depressed that day and I shouldn't have made that your problem.

ANITA. No, that's all right. (*SHE starts to pick up books.*) You know, a lot of people are not really sure you're dying.

RAVENSWAAL. (*Interested*) Who?

ANITA. Me and my friends.

RAVENSWAAL. Your friends? They're doctors?

ANITA. No. Two are from shipping, one's a receptionist. We were talking how a number of times on TV somebody is told they're dying, and it's a mix-up of the X-rays. Once even on the "Honeymooners," Jackie Gleason *heard* he was dying, but it was his mother-in-law's cocker spaniel. And they told Gleason he was gonna get sick and lay by the stove and drink warm milk from a saucer. And when he found out it was a cocker spaniel, did they laugh. Maybe that's what happened to you.

(*Pause. RAVENSWAAL stares at her a moment in disbelief Calmly HE raises his eyes to the ceiling*)

RAVENSWAAL. Are you listening to this?

ANITA. That's nice, you talk to God.

RAVENSWAAL. When he talks back we've got something.

ANITA. It's good though ... in case you're really dying. He could get you into heaven. He could put you on the good list.

RAVENSWAAL. You know all about heaven?

ANITA. Sure. I'm a Catholic. The nuns told me.

RAVENSWAAL. Tell me about it.

ANITA. (*Reacts.*) Tell you? You know.

RAVENSWAAL. (*Putting her on HE crosses*) I'm old now. I forget things. Tell me the whole story. Dying, heaven, the "good" list, everything.

ANITA. (*Enthusiastic.*) Oh, it's wonderful. First you die.

RAVENSWAAL. A given.

ANITA. Then your soul leaves your body.

RAVENSWAAL. My soul?

ANITA. Yeah. It looks like you only you can see through it.

RAVENSWAAL. Okay. I'm out of my body. A floating transparency.

ANITA. And then you start to go up. (*Getting into it*) Higher than the stars. And then you come to the gates. And then he meets you.

RAVENSWAAL. Who?

ANITA. Well, St. Peter meets the Catholics.

RAVENSWAAL. I'm an Agnostic.

ANITA. Oh. I'm sure they got someone around who meets Agnostics Anyway, they check the list. And the good list goes to heaven, and the bad list goes to ... we don't want to get into that right now ... (*Wistful.*) And when you get to heaven, everybody is there, like your parents and they're not mad at you anymore and they tell you that they really love you and they don't hit you anymore. (*Pause. A thought.*) Oh. Be sure to wear warm clothes to heaven.

RAVENSWAAL. A nun told you that?

ANITA. No, Mrs. LiCausi. She was there.

RAVENSWAAL. Where?

ANITA. In heaven! Mrs. LiCausi was there once for one minute.

RAVENSWAAL. A whole group went? Club Med? What are you talking about?!

ANITA. No. I'll tell you the whole story. Mrs. LiCausi went to Orchard Beach with her son, Paulie—I hated him. He had ringworm and he only had hair on one side of his head—and he was always rubbing—(*SHE rubs side of her head*)

RAVENSWAAL. Short! Short!

ANITA. I'm sorry. Anyway, she went to Orchard Beach and she went in the water too *soon* after eating a sausage and cheese sandwich ... she loved her provolone. (*RAVENSWAAL taps his cane on the floor to hurry her up*) Sooooooo, she started to drown. The lifeguard pulled her out and gave her mouth-to-mouth and brought her back to life. (*Dramatic. To center*) And she told us that while she was dead for one minute, she went to heaven. And in heaven, she was walking through a long tunnel, towards a door. And in the tunnel she was very cold, 'cause she only had on a bathing suit. So she said, when it's time for me to die, I should bundle up. (*To him.*) So, that's all you need to worry about. Other than that, heaven is terrific. Make you feel better?

(SHE leans down to him as SHE finishes. HE gently raises his hand to find her head, then suddenly pulls her hair)

ANITA. Ow! You hurt my hair!
RAVENSWAAL. I'm sorry. I'm very sorry. I've never done anything like that. *(Trying to regain control of himself)*
ANITA. Then why'd you do it?
RAVENSWAAL. It's the way you think. The dog's X-rays, Mrs. LiCausi running around heaven in a wet bathing suit. Those are just pat, smug, easy answers to *questions* that have *consumed* the thoughts of the greatest minds of every generation. It's astrology, it's cult worship, it's .
ANITA. I thought it was hope.

(Pause)

RAVENSWAAL Hope! Read. Read or go home Baudelaire.
ANITA. Which Baudelaire? There's two.
RAVENSWAAL. The Poems!

(SHE picks up a bunch of books, then glares at him Suddenly SHE walks deliberately over to him and silently makes funny, ugly faces at him HE senses she is doing something but doesn't know what it is Satisfied that SHE has silently insulted him, SHE goes and sits down on the straight-back chair at stage right SHE puts other books under chair, then reads

Baudelaire. SHE reads from a book-marked spot. SHE doesn't read terribly well, but competently.)

ANITA. (*Reading*) "The Clock. The Clock. Terrible Clock! God without mercy, mighty power! Saying all day, Remember and beware." (*Stops reading and yells to him.*) You're lucky Dominic doesn't know you pulled my hair. (*Reads*) "There is no arrow of pain but in a tiny hour. Will make thy heart—" (*Stops reading.*) He'd break your knees with a baseball bat. (*Reads.*) "Will make thy heart its target and stick and vibrate there towards the horizon—" (*Still angry.*) Dominic's my boyfriend you know. Since the eighth grade. (*Reads.*) "Toward the horizon all too soon and out of sight." (*Begins to sniffle SHE is holding back tears.*) "Vaporous pleasure ..."

(SHE gets up to get tissues SHE is no longer able to read RAVENSWAAL refuses to acknowledge her anguish SHE continues to try and not cry, but finally tears come)

ANITA. Who knows where he is. He could be hanging on a meat hook somewhere, his guts ripped out ... "Vaporous pleasure" ... (*Then through her tears, SHE takes tissues and blows her nose)*

RAVENSWAAL. (*Sighs)* Young lady, I know at this point, it is expected of me to feign interest in that which is obviously distressing you. I will not. In whatever *number* of days I have remaining, I am determined to *occupy myself* with the great beauty which I will soon never hear again. My time is too precious to investigate this tale of yours, which sounds both hideous and banal at the same time. Please take a moment to compose yourself or we'll have to call it a day.

ANITA (*Composing herself*) I'm sorry. I'll read. (*Looks for her place.*) It's just that the last time I saw him, he was jumping out a window in his underwear ... Oh, never mind.

(*SHE finds her place, and starts to read HE seems to be listening calmly*)

ANITA. "Vaporous pleasure like a syl .. syl ..." I don't know how to say this word. (*Spells.*) S -Y-L-P-H-I-

RAVENSWAAL. It's no use.

ANITA. No, if you just help me ...

RAVENSWAAL. No. I'm sitting here thinking, "Why did he jump out the window in his underwear?"

ANITA. Oh Mr. Ravenswaal, it was terrible! Last month we were—(*Sincere*) You don't want to hear my problems.

RAVENSWAAL. (*Waves to her to come over to him*) I can't concentrate. Tell me!

ANITA Okay. I haven't seen Dominic in three weeks. I have this apartment. It's almost a three, but it's really a two-and-a-half, the fridge is in the living room.

RAVENSWAAL. Please ... (*HE raps cane on floor to hurry her*)

ANITA. Okay, *short*. So Dominic was sleeping over that night. We do that sometimes. We're still *just* engaged, but we ... you know.

RAVENSWAAL. I approve.

ANITA. Thank you. I heard a noise in the other room...

RAVENSWAAL. Dominic didn't hear it?

ANITA. I had his ears covered ... (*Giggles at the memory, then hesitates to explain.*) He likes me to ...

RAVENSWAAL. (*A beat*) Go on, go on.

ANITA. (*Slowly, to build the tension.*) I went out in the living room ...

RAVENSWAAL. With the fridge, yes!

ANITA. And just then a shotgun blew off my front door.

RAVENSWAAL. What?

ANITA. (*Nods.*) Yeah, and two guys with ski masks burst in. I screamed. They ran for the bedroom and got there just as Dominic was going out the window. They shot at him, but I saw he got away. So they punched me in the stomach and tried to rape me. Anyway, it's been three weeks now. I don't know if he's alive—

RAVENSWAAL. They tried to rape you?

ANITA. Yeah. But the police came and they ran.

RAVENSWAAL Thank God.

ANITA. Yeah Only then the police got mad because I wouldn't tell them where Dominic was so one of them shoved me on the floor and they left. What a night. I couldn't get back to sleep. I was tossing and turning and ...

RAVENSWAAL. (*Frustrated*) Wait a minute Go back! You were beaten and nearly raped!

ANITA. I know I was there.... You're not getting the point.

RAVENSWAAL. I got the point. The point is, this fiancé of yours got himself into some kind of extreme jeopardy and rather than face the consequences of his unsavory actions, he abandoned you to be beaten and raped.

ANITA. (*Thinks a minute.*) You got the wrong point. My point is, we love each other and I miss him and I'm worried about him.

RAVENSWAAL. You're worried. Who worries about you?

ANITA. I'm okay. You know, I feel better that I got it off my chest. Thank you. (*Picks up book, sits.*) Back to Baudelaire.

RAVENSWAAL. I'm afraid that your little anecdote has rendered poetry temporarily irrelevant.

ANITA. I'm sorry. (*Then to make up, SHE grabs a book from under chair and whispers.*) Psst. You want me to read from the *special* book?

RAVENSWAAL. (*Whispers back.*) Oh, all right. Yes.

ANITA. (*Starts reading.*) "Leland cupped my breast in his hand before he even said 'Hello.' Leland, I thought, was someone to be reckoned with. As his tongue darted between my half-parted lips I was no longer aware of anyone else in the whole restaurant ... I knew he cared for me ...

RAVENSWAAL. (*Interrupting.*) Wait a minute, I know why you don't like to think about sex. The boyfriend jumped out the window three weeks ago and since then you have no outlet for your physical urges. Correct?

ANITA. Right.

RAVENSWAAL. (*Smiles*) I broke the code ... Thank you very much. Go on.

ANITA. (*Reads.*) "I knew I was powerless to deny him whatever his hot throbbing loins required." Whew. "I accepted that he was total master as he slipped beneath the table. His hand searched my calf, then my thigh, then ..."

*(Quietly, the NURSE enters ANITA is aware of her, and
hiding the book, SHE, without hesitation begins ad-
libbing the other book as if reading.)*

ANITA. Tick-tock where's my clock said Baudelaire.
Remember, remember.
RAVENSWAAL. What the hell—
NURSE. Mr. Ravenswaal, you're scheduled for X-rays
in ten minutes. If you don't come nicely, I'll get Raul to
drag you. *(NURSE exits, staring back oddly at Anita.)*
ANITA. She's gone.
RAVENSWAAL. Oh, very clever thinking, Anita. You
demonstrated a grace under pressure seldom found amongst
the abysmally ignorant.
ANITA. I didn't want her to know we read that stuff.
RAVENSWAAL. *(Sincere apology.)* I'm sorry. I didn't
mean that.
ANITA. That's all right.
RAVENSWAAL. Apparently my skills in the social
graces have degenerated at the same rate as my kidneys.

*(HE goes into the bathroom SHE goes to his closet and
looks through his clothes)*

ANITA. How come you got no visitors?
RAVENSWAAL. *(Offstage.)* Have no visitors.
ANITA. How come you *have* no visitors?
RAVENSWAAL. *(Offstage.)* I don't know anybody.
ANITA. When did your wife die?
RAVENSWAAL. *(Off, surprised)* Did I *tell* you my
wife died?
ANITA. *(Caught)* Uh ... yeah .

RAVENSWAAL. (*Offstage.*) No, I didn't.

ANITA. No, you didn't *tell* me. I figured it out. You got a wedding ring and uh ... you know, she's not here, so...

RAVENSWAAL. (*Offstage.*) Oh ... good work, Holmes.

(FLUSHING sound from bathroom.)

ANITA. Holmes? ... Oh, Sherlock Holmes! (*Enjoys it, then crosses and sits on window sill*) Hey ... that's a good one.

RAVENSWAAL. (*Enters from bathroom.*) She died a year ago.

ANITA. Any children?

RAVENSWAAL. (*Pause*) No. "My students were my children." That's from *Goodbye Mr. Chips* What an idiot he was.

ANITA. Did you try?

RAVENSWAAL. No. We were teachers. We were waiting till we achieved financial security.

ANITA. No friends?

RAVENSWAAL. None.

ANITA. That's a lie.

RAVENSWAAL. I beg your pardon.

ANITA. The head nurse told me. A couple of people came to see you. Your old students. Another teacher. Why don't you let them come up?

RAVENSWAAL. I'm too busy.

ANITA. Come on.

RAVENSWAAL. "When a man takes to his bed, many of his friends have a secret desire to see him die; some to prove that his health is inferior to their own, others in the hope of being able to study a death agony."

ANITA. Ick. Where'd you hear that?

RAVENSWAAL. (*Laughs.*) Baudelaire. The same man who wrote, "Tick-tock, where the hell's my clock?"

ANITA. Didn't you have, like, favorite students? Teacher's pets?

RAVENSWAAL. You mean like Ben Weinstein?

ANITA. He was your favorite student?

RAVENSWAAL. No. He was one of my colleagues. He was dean at Hofstra before me. *He* had favorites. What a funeral they had for him. The wailing, the weeping. Over a thousand students showed up. He of course had the funeral on a *school* day.

ANITA. Was he a good teacher?

RAVENSWAAL. What he knew about Chaucer you could stick in your eye and not have to blink for ten years.

ANITA. But they must have liked him.

RAVENSWAAL. (*Crosses and sits on the stage right chair she was sitting on There are books under this chair*) Of *course* they liked him. He dedicated his life to being popular ... I, on the other hand, dedicated *my* life to holding people to a rigid standard of intellectual honesty .. which should make for a sparse gathering at my grave-side. No, the only students who could visit me are those who have a pathological need to *behave* well.

ANITA. But you educated them. That's a splendid thing.

RAVENSWAAL Is it? I don't know. Do you see any evidence that the various institutions of higher learning have raised anything higher—other than tuition?

ANITA. It's not something you can see but it's there. It's like—me and my girlfriend Lenore once went to a college football game. She was dating the coach. He was a nice looking guy, except that he had all this hair on his back. He was always rubbing ...

(SHE rubs the back of her neck as HE taps his cane on the floor to hurry her up)

ANITA. And we sat up in the card section and on a signal we each had to hold up a different colored card to *make a picture* And the people across the way, went, "Oooh." But we couldn't see what we were holding up. But it must have been a beautiful picture 'cause everyone was going, "Oooh." "Oooh." "Ahh." "Ahh." "Ayy." ...

(RAVENSWAAL bangs his cane on the floor)

ANITA. Turns out it was a big orange duck. Go figure.

RAVENSWAAL. An insipid story for any occasion. What you're saying is, that like the people in the card section, I'm not *privileged* to see the fruits of my labor. But that I should be proud that I held up my card.

ANITA. *(Delighted)* *This* is when it's fun talking with you, 'cause you are quick. *(Snapping her fingers, SHE sits, punctuating "quick")*

RAVENSWAAL. *(More serious)* I accept your accolade. I am *proud* to have held up my card. Far too many people do not. But it's not enough. Before I go, I want to see the picture. I want to know *why* I was holding up my card. I want to know the purpose of my existence. I want to see the duck. (*HE stands almost tripping on the books under the chair*)

ANITA. All right. Sit down. Watch those books. I'm gonna tell you what you didn't see. The whole meaning of life.

RAVENSWAAL. This should be good.

ANITA. I learned it while I was working at the Museum of Natural History.

RAVENSWAAL. (*Startled*) You were a guide?

ANITA. Waitress. In the cafeteria. The "Descent of Man" display was right opposite the ladies' toilet, so I saw it twice a day. Do you know we used to be bugs? Then we were fish, then lungfish, then animals, then apes, then people. And the display said that evolution is still going on today, only too slow for us to see it. (*SHE pauses to think.*)

RAVENSWAAL. You're right, I feel much better.

ANITA. (*Yells.*) Hold it a minute. I'm in the middle of a thought here. Now get this: If in the last billion years we went from bugs to people, where are we gonna go the next billion years? Hah?

RAVENSWAAL. I can't imagine.

ANITA. ... Angels! (*Nods wisely*) At one end is little bugs in the ocean and way off at the other end where we're going are angels. Now some of us, you know the type that talk to you on buses? They're lagging behind closer to the bugs and the apes, and the others like the guys who wrote these books ... are closer to the angels.

RAVENSWAAL. Angels.

ANITA. Yeah, angels.

RAVENSWAAL. (*Waving book.*) I hate to play the cynic, but an *incredible number* of these "angels" list among their achievements, psychosis, alcoholism, drug addiction, and that old favorite, mister syphilis. Angels.

ANITA. (*Grabs book.*) I didn't say they acted like angels. They didn't get that far yet. I just meant they were close enough to hear them. I mean, I get up in the morning, I *think:* "I gotta get new pantyhose, what'll I have for lunch, should I get a new headboard." ... And these people get up and *think;* "Maybe I'll write how it feels to look at a sunset." Most of us don't get to hear the angels— we're out buying headboards—so we listen to these people—and that's how we know that the angels are there. And we can't get there unless guys like you who love this stuff, hold up your card. And that's the picture. (*Pause, SHE sits.*) Huh?

RAVENSWAAL. They hear the angels ... then you would postulate that this is how a deaf Beethoven could write his "Ode to Joy"? In fact, you would argue, that God *made* him deaf so he would hear nothing *but* angels.

ANITA. (*Agrees happily.*) There you go. Quick again.

RAVENSWAAL. You know, when Darwin first presented his theory of evolution we listened, then looked around at each other, examined our behavior and said, "He's right, we're just better looking baboons." How sad that it seemed so unassailably logical. But there is a giant flaw in the concept of evolution. (*Pause.*) What is it, you wonder.

ANITA. I do.

RAVENSWAAL. Evolution is disgustingly simple. Creatures maintain the characteristics which help them survive and discard the characteristics that are no value in survival. A fish develops a lung, *it* can go on land and have a less restricted food supply. Ergo, it survives. A fish *doesn't* develop a gallbladder, an ear, a penis—all fine organs in their own right ... but of no use to your average fish. Nature saves those for a creature that will need them to survive. Now. Here is the flaw—(*HE taps her head*)

ANITA. Me ...

RAVENSWAAL. No. The human brain. *Why* did nature give us this? It isn't necessary. Oh, of course, it's necessary for us to have some cerebrum so that we can function. But if man had developed a brain only slightly more complex than that of a gorilla, he could have ruled his environment quite adequately. So why?! Why was *he* given this incredible mechanism that he did not need for survival? And the answer is ... we don't know.

ANITA. (*Disappointed.*) AWWW.

RAVENSWAAL. Is the human race just an evolutionary blunder? A wrong turn, say ... at lungfish? Or could it be, could it possibly be, Anita, that there *is* a grander plan for the universe, and that the apotheosis of human achievement is *not* jet travel, heart transplants, the hydrogen bomb, or even call-waiting ... But that this amazing organ *was* purposely put here so that some day we could actually achieve a grace and a glory that would allow us to look at each other, examine our behavior and then think the unthinkable, that we are indeed touched by the angels.

ANITA. (*Sings.*) Ave Maria ....

RAVENSWAAL. (*Turns to her surprised.*) What happened, did a nun walk in here?

ANITA. (*Stops singing and stands.*) I'm sorry. That was so inspiring. And so many words in a row. How do you think of all that so fast?

RAVENSWAAL. It's not so fast. That's more or less the same lecture I used to give the first day of every semester. You gave me an opening to do it again, so I jumped right in and took it. You might have noticed I like to hear myself talk. However, you're the first person who ever sang.

ANITA. (*Sits in chair under TV.*) I got so excited to find out you believe what I believe. That means we see the same picture.

RAVENSWAAL. (*Condescending.*) No. I said it every semester. I never believed it. It was just my annual "Art As Religion" speech

ANITA. But you're a teacher. Why would you try to convince your students of something you don't believe?

RAVENSWAAL. I wasn't trying to convince them. I was trying to convince me. Do you know, I once took a book—it was Immanuel Kant—and I literally pressed it against a student's face, so convinced was I that if he could only *integrate it* into his thinking, it would uplift the quality of his life and of those lives he would touch. And now .. as I reach out for the truth, and the beauty that I know exists in literature and music, *I find that it* means as much to me as it would to one of your bugs that was about to be stepped on. Anita, I would *trade* all I know for the ability to believe in Mrs. LiCausi's heaven, because what I do believe offers me no solace. How can I let my students come up here and tell them that all the wisdom we shared in the classroom has left me sitting here feeling nothing but alone. I'm afraid, Anita. I'm just afraid.

(SHE goes to him obviously shaken by what she has just heard SHE goes to touch his shoulder, but is interrupted by the NURSE. SHE has a wheelchair.)

NURSE. Okay, Mr. Ravenswaal, we're off to X-ray. Do you get in the chair or do I call Raul? (*HE gets into the wheelchair*)

RAVENSWAAL. I'm coming. I'm coming.

NURSE. Watch the foot pedals. The braille teacher is here today, do you want me to send her to your room ...

RAVENSWAAL. No.

NURSE. There's a musical program in the cafeteria for patients tonight. Do you want to go?

RAVENSWAAL. No.

NURSE. Do you need to urinate?

RAVENSWAAL. I'll wait until we get in the elevator.

NURSE. (*Wheeling him off.*) You're no day at the beach, Mr. Ravenswaal.

(*THEY exit, leaving ANITA standing alone and thoughtful*)

(*LIGHTS dim to BLACK*)

Scene 3

Another day It is early evening around seven o'clock. MR. RAVENSWAAL is asleep in bed. The radio-cassette is on, playing BEETHOVEN'S NINTH The door opens and ANITA enters SHE is wearing a rather revealing dress

ANITA. Hi.

(No response ANITA comes closer and realizes that HE's sleeping SHE makes a disappointed noise and, slightly upset, turns off RADIO. The NURSE rushes in SHE's carrying a cup of water and pill.)

NURSE. *(Calling into hall.)* I'll be right there, wait for me. *(To Ravenswaal.)* Okay, here's your pill— *(Disappointed)* Aaaah.

ANITA. He's sleeping.

NURSE *(Notices Anita.)* Sleeping. They send me with a pain pill for a man who's sleeping. This place is a joke. *(SHE turns to leave)*

ANITA. Wait. You're not going to wake him? What if he sleeps for hours?

NURSE. It's good for him. Don't you come on Fridays?

ANITA. *(Uncomfortable)* Yeah, usually ... but ...

NURSE. *(New thought.)* Hey, you want to come to a party?

ANITA. Where?

NURSE. Physical Therapy. Doctor Binder's birthday. They say he's about a hundred years old. Come on, you're dressed for a party.

ANITA. *(SHE crosses to his bedside.)* No. I've got to talk to Mr. Ravenswaal. How long does he normally sleep?

NURSE. *(Smiles.)* Look, if you want, I'll wake him. It's kinda fun.

ANITA. Go ahead.

(NURSE goes to wake him by pulling his nose. ANITA suddenly stops her)

ANITA. No.

(The NURSE stops.)

NURSE. What?
ANITA. *(Thinking)* Uh—you go to your party. I'll give him his pill.
NURSE. *(Serious)* You're not a nurse.
ANITA. It goes in his mouth, right?
NURSE. Yes.
ANITA. I'll give him his pill .. in his mouth.
NURSE. *(Gives Anita pill)* Well, okay. The water's over there. If you change your mind the party's down the hall—If he asks, tell him his radio was stolen—Raul ... I got music!

(The NURSE exits with the radio; but during the above checks his audio cassette and leaves it behind ANITA puts the pill down and goes back to the door SHE looks furtively up and down the hall, then closes the door. SHE stares at Ravenswaal, then drags his straight-back chair in front of the door so it can't be opened from the outside SHE comes over to the bed. SHE is obviously worried SHE is deciding what to do. SHE reaches a decision and comes right up next to him. SHE leans over him and starts to nibble around his ear.
HE stirs, but doesn't wake After another brief hesitation, SHE continues and begins to gently stroke his chest. RAVENSWAAL begins to stir more actively and then begins to emit satisfied noises SHE continues to kiss the area around his ear and seductively rub his chest as SHE opens a button on his pajama top

*RAVENSWAAL wakes up and stops making noises.
HE's confused
SHE rubs a little lower)*

RAVENSWAAL. Are you a new nurse?

*(SHE doesn't answer. SHE kisses and rubs, HE alternates
between satisfaction and confusion.)*

RAVENSWAAL. Mmm ... mmh ... who? ... mm ... I
would enjoy this a lot more if I knew who you were.

*(HE tries to touch her—SHE slaps him away. SHE kisses
him on the chest and her hand disappears under the
covers HE reacts, startled but excited. SHE continues)*

RAVENSWAAL. No, really, stop. I have to have a
name, some conversation ... Ooooh! No, stop!

*(HE grabs for her SHE pulls away, causing him to almost
tumble out of the bed HE cries out.)*

RAVENSWAAL. Security! Raul! Help!
ANITA. Mr. Ravenswaal! Oh, geez, are you all right?
RAVENSWAAL. Anita? My God, someone was just in
here. You have no idea what she did to me. I was sound
asleep and the next thing I knew ... *(Realizes)* Anita?
ANITA. *(Quietly)* Yeah ...
RAVENSWAAL. You? ...
ANITA *(A little shy)* Uh-huh. Are you mad at me?
RAVENSWAAL. No, I'm confused. We met, we read,
we had a few brief discussions ... then we're suddenly

hurled into intimacy. We seem to have left out courtship. Speak to me, say something.

ANITA. I need three hundred dollars.

RAVENSWAAL *(Laughs)* AHH! Poetry prepares you for *nothing*!

ANITA. *(Sincere)* I really need that money. It's a matter of life and death I know people always say that, but this really is.

RAVENSWAAL. Will you get me my robe, please? I'm not prepared to dispute the magnitude of your need. But why didn't you walk in here and ask me for the money?

ANITA. *(SHE helps him put on his robe.)* I was too embarrassed.

RAVENSWAAL. *(Attacking)* Oh, you were embarrassed to be thought of as a beggar. So you chose to handle the situation in a more dignified manner.

ANITA. I'm sorry. I didn't think you'd give me so much money for nothing. I mean, we hardly know each other.

RAVENSWAAL. But we certainly took a giant step today!

ANITA. Okay I made a mistake Big deal. I needed help, I figured this was a way.

RAVENSWAAL. Quite a way! Having intercourse with a dying, sleeping, blind man.

ANITA. *(Offended)* I wasn't gonna have intercourse! What are you, crazy?!

RAVENSWAAL. What was this a prelude to?

ANITA. You know   the other.

RAVENSWAAL. What other?

ANITA. The other thing that guys like.

RAVENSWAAL. Which one?

ANITA. (*Upset.*) There's only two. You know ... I don't like to say it.

RAVENSWAAL. Are we talking about fellatio?

ANITA. (*Confused*) Maybe.

RAVENSWAAL. (*Impatiently.*) Are we talking about oral sex?

ANITA. Oral sex. Yeah. I'm sorry. I'm stupid ... I even put on a sexy dress and you're blind. See, I *was* gonna talk it over with you first, but when I found you sleeping, I figured I'd just do something and you'd wake up and then somehow we'd get around to the money ... it's dumb, I'm dumb ... you're smart, say something. (*SHE sits on the chair blocking the door*)

RAVENSWAAL. (*A beat*) At my wife's funeral, in a *moment* of—I think understandable —depression, I *embraced* my second cousin, Lois, who until that time had never been *more to me* than a scrawled signature on a Christmas card In the six seconds that my head was buried in her mouton coat, Lois *decided* that we had become friends for life. Soul mates. This led to her calling me every day for four-and-a-half months to discuss a gamut of fascinating topics such as whether she should paint or wallpaper the bathroom.

ANITA. (*Arch*) Short! Short!

RAVENSWAAL. (*Heads for bathroom.*) What I'm trying to say is that we should keep *things on* a formal basis. We didn't, and that's what's led to today's humiliation. There is no reason for us to have any but the most perfunctory relationship. You're here as a reader. Read.

ANITA. Which—

RAVENSWAAL. Read the Keats. The one you were reading last time.

(ANITA *takes a book and opens it to a marked spot HE goes into the bathroom)*

ANITA. (*Reads a little better.*) *When I Have Fears That I May Cease To Be.* Oh, yeah. Here's another one of your jolly favorites.
"When I have fears that I may cease to be
Before my pen has glean'd my teeming brain,
Before High-piled books in charact'ry
Hold like rich garners the full-ripen'd grain;"
RAVENSWAAL. (*Re-enters.*) You're pregnant.
ANITA. Huh?
RAVENSWAAL. The three hundred dollars. It's because you're pregnant.
ANITA. No, it's Dominic.
RAVENSWAAL. Ah! The one on the meat hook.
ANITA. It turns out he wasn't on a meat hook. He called me. He's living inside an oil drum in New Jersey.
RAVENSWAAL. He needs money to redecorate? I'm sorry, go on.
ANITA. You see, I first met Dominic when I was twelve, he was—
RAVENSWAAL. Twelve! My God we're starting this story from twelve! Try to remember I'm under severe time pressure.
ANITA. Oh, yeah. You want your pain pill?
RAVENSWAAL. No. Just some water please.

ANITA (*Brings his water.*) Okay. I just wanted you to know how long I've known Dominic, so you'd know how important he is to me.

RAVENSWAAL. You're giving me a rich history. Very Dickensian.

ANITA. Thank you very much. Anyway, Dominic's been out of work a lot. So he got his part-time job beating up people. (*SHE takes water and returns it to night table*)

RAVENSWAAL. He got this through an agency?

ANITA. No, through a couple of guys. You know.

RAVENSWAAL. I know, I know ...

ANITA So they sent him to beat up a guy. Guess what? He beat up the wrong guy. But he's not dumb. They sent him to beat up Milo Vuckovich. But he beat up Frankie Vuckovich. On the doorbell it said F. Vuckovich and Dominic thought the F was for "Fats" which is what they call Milo.

(*RAVENSWAAL smiles and a small laugh bursts out of him*)

ANITA. Well, didn't you ever make a mistake like that?

RAVENSWAAL. I can't count the number of times I've accidently beaten up a guy named Fats.

ANITA. He beat up Frankie. Who is a very important man ... Anyway, there's this guy, George, from Newark, who Dommy met when they pulled George's cousin, Nunzio, out of a pizza oven ...

RAVENSWAAL. (*Interrupts*) That story *alone* is worth three hundred dollars.

ANITA. (*Snaps*) Please let me finish. If Dominic gives George the three hundred dollars he owes him, George will square it with Frankie, then all Dommy has to do is leave town. Otherwise, they'll kill him and we won't be able to get married. I'm sorry I asked.

RAVENSWAAL. In my inside coat pocket in the closet you should find my checkbook.

ANITA. (*SHE reacts.*) You're sure?

RAVENSWAAL. Why not? I'm not leaving my money to cousin Lois.

(ANITA goes to the closet)

RAVENSWAAL. You'll have to fill it out. I'll sign my name as best I can.

ANITA. (*Returns and starts to happily fill out the check)* Thank you Mr. Ravenswaal. I'm so glad I didn't have to ask Bobby or Mister Forrester. (*Realizes)* Bobby's a salesman where I work and Mr. Forrester is my boss.

RAVENSWAAL. Were you going to ask them the same way you asked me?

ANITA. Huh? Oh, you mean—what was that big word for that?

RAVENSWAAL. Fellatio.

ANITA. Isn't that a pretty word? (*Back on track.*) Yeah, I guess that's what I would've done.

RAVENSWAAL. Don't you think that asking your boss *for money* in exchange for sexual favors could have unfortunate ramifications?

ANITA. Probably. I mean I never asked for money any of the other times I did it for him. What's today's date?

RAVENSWAAL Hold it. Back up! Back up. Any of the other times you did *what* for him?

ANITA. Fellatio.

RAVENSWAAL. You do that with your boss?

ANITA. Not all the time.

RAVENSWAAL. How often?

ANITA. Just once in awhile.

RAVENSWAAL. What business is this man in?

ANITA. Water.

RAVENSWAAL. He's a lifeguard? What?!

ANITA. Lifeguard? No (*SHE laughs.*) Deer Park, water. Bottled water. He doesn't own the whole thing. He just runs this one plant. I check the caps on the bottles. You know the red little plastic ...

RAVENSWAAL. (*Interrupts.*) Are you sleeping with this man, are you having an affair, is it something your union is trying to stop?

ANITA. (*As if to a child.*) Mr. Forrester is married. *I'm* engaged to Dominic. I wouldn't sleep with my boss. I just go into his office sometimes and give him a little fun. What *is* the date?

RAVENSWAAL. The seventeenth! And if not money, what does Mr. Forrester give you?

ANITA. I get the best hours. I get the best vacations. He sees I'm never hassled by the foreman or any of the guys. You know, it's hard for a single woman in a plant like that.

RAVENSWAAL. So you're fighting sexual harassment with fellatio. (*HE sits.*)

ANITA. Hey, it works for me. Should I show you where to sign? (*SHE gives him the checkbook and pen.*)

RAVENSWAAL. And this salesman Bobby? You do the same with him?

ANITA. No! He ... (*A little shy.*) He likes me. Bobby's a nice kid. He puts flowers on my chair. I couldn't do it with him. He'd get all serious ...

(*RAVENSWAAL throws down checkbook.*)

ANITA. (*Worried.*) What? You changed your mind ...
RAVENSWAAL I think I signed the check "Fellatio."
ANITA. (*Looks*) Yeah you did. This'd be pretty hard to cash.
RAVENSWAAL. Make out another one.

(*ANITA begins to make out a new check SOMEONE attempts to open the room door The door bangs against the chair that's blocking it*)

NURSE. (*Offstage*) Hey, what's going on?
ANITA. Just a second.
NURSE. Open this door I'm a nurse!

(*ANITA hurries to finish filling out the check and hands it to Ravenswaal. SHE jumps up to move chair from door The NURSE enters SHE is suspicious and carrying a small paper plate with cake SHE wears a party hat. RAVENSWAAL is signing the check*)

NURSE. I brought you some cake. Why did you block the door?
ANITA. It was an accident.
NURSE. The chair got there by accident?
ANITA. (*Moving it back*) It's back. Okay?
NURSE. What were you doing?

ANITA. Reading. What do you think we were doing?
RAVENSWAAL. Here's your check, Anita.

(ANITA takes the check. The NURSE tries to look at it. ANITA hides it from her.)

NURSE. (*Leeringly.*) I guess the real party was going on down here.
ANITA. (*Tough.*) Look. I don't care what you were thinking. But if you say what you're thinking, you could go from a nurse to a patient in one second.
NURSE. (*Indignant*) Oh perfect. I came down here like a nice person with cake, and I get yelled at! I just try to be cheerful so people like him won't be depressed about dying. (*Putting the plate on bed, the NURSE walks out.*)
RAVENSWAAL. That girl has been a great comfort to me.
ANITA. She's gonna tell everybody what we didn't do. I gotta get this money to Dominic—he's gonna be so excited. Here, she brought this for you. *Mangia (Hands him the cake)*
RAVENSWAAL. We're not reading anymore?
ANITA. Well, it's not really my "read" day. I came tonight special, to ... discuss my problem. Tomorrow's my "read" day
RAVENSWAAL. Right, right. You're coming tomorrow?

(Pause)

ANITA. I don't know.
RAVENSWAAL. (*Nervous*) What do you mean?

ANITA. Well, I don't know Dominic's plans. I don't know if he's coming back here, or when, or if we're coming back together ... or if we're gonna have to leave the *country* ...

RAVENSWAAL. You mean you might never come back?

ANITA. I don't know. (*Nice.*) You're gonna miss me?

RAVENSWAAL. Miss you? What are you talking about? I just don't want to sit here like a fool waiting for a reader who isn't coming. Anita, don't take this personally, but if you don't come back, it's probably *better* for me anyway. I really don't have the time or energy to deal with any of this nonsense you call your life. I've tried to make polite conver ... what the hell am I eating here?! (*HE starts to pull something stringy from his mouth.*)

ANITA. It's Doctor Binder's birthday cake.

RAVENSWAAL. It's got a worm in it.

ANITA. No. I think it's part of the cake decoration. A toy stethoscope or something . ... I gotta go now... (*Starts to kiss his forehead but stops.*) I don't know how to thank you, Mr. Ravenswaal, 'cause what I want more than anything in the world is to marry Dominic. I'll miss you (*SHE goes to door carrying string from cake.*)

RAVENSWAAL. (*A little scared.*) Anita?

ANITA. (*Returns to throw "string" in trash.*) I'm still here.

RAVENSWAAL. Oh. I still didn't get an answer. How do I know if you're coming tomorrow?

ANITA. (*Gentle.*) If I'm not coming, I'll call. Is that okay?

RAVENSWAAL. Okay. And if I'm not here, I went skiing.

ANITA. That's a good one Mr. Ravenswaal.

*(SHE laughs and exits. HE sits still for a moment, then
    angrily turns the cake upside down on the table.
We hear BEETHOVEN'S NINTH.
LIGHTS fade out.)*

End of ACT I

ACT II

*The Next day mid-morning. We hear BEETHOVEN'S
NINTH until LIGHTS are full up, then music fades out.
Ravenswaal's room is empty. The door is open We
hear RAVENSWAAL being very pleasant*

RAVENSWAAL. (*Offstage*) Good morning. Good
morning all.
NURSE. Do you want to check in on Mr. Santoni?
RAVENSWAAL. Yes, let's continue our stroll down
bedpan alley.

(THEY get to Santoni's door)

NURSE. Here we are.
RAVENSWAAL. Good morning Mr. Santoni You
have such wonderful color today ...
NURSE. Now, we're heading back home ...
RAVENSWAAL. I have the best nurse, she's a young
Mother Teresa.

*(MR RAVENSWAAL and the NURSE appear in
doorway SHE's holding his arm, and has his radio
under her other arm HE pulls away in mid-sentence and
is his cranky self)*

51

RAVENSWAAL All right. I ambulated. I exercised. I chatted with the doomed—Who was that man who patted me on the head and told me to "Hang in there"?

NURSE. That was Miss Jessup of the Red Cross.

RAVENSWAAL. A woman? SHE sounded like Winston Churchill.

NURSE. She's English.

RAVENSWAAL. I'm not talking about her accent, I'm talking about a serious hormonal imbalance.

NURSE. She was nice. She gave you soap and a washcloth.

RAVENSWAAL. I didn't appreciate the implication.

NURSE. (*Lying.*) Good news, Mr. Ravenswaal ... They found your radio. I caught the girl who stole it. It's right here on the night table. (*Then*) I'll be right back.

RAVENSWAAL. Wait!

NURSE. What?

RAVENSWAAL. We struck a quid pro quo.

NURSE. A what?

RAVENSWAAL. A bargain. I'd walk, you'd make the call. (*Reluctantly, SHE goes to the phone and takes out a piece of paper from her pocket*)

NURSE. Oh yeah.

RAVENSWAAL. Do you have the right number?

NURSE. I got it from information. There was only one Anita Merendino. 554 West 53rd Street. That's it, right?

RAVENSWAAL. I don't know. It's the one with the door blown off.

(*Pause.*)

NURSE. There's no answer.

RAVENSWAAL. Let it ring.

NURSE. I can't stand here all day ... I have *things* to do.

RAVENSWAAL. All right, hang up. Call the Deer Park Water Company.

NURSE. I'm a nurse, not a secretary.

RAVENSWAAL. Forget it. I'll do it myself. Go.

NURSE. Fine. (*SHE starts out*) Boy, whatever she did with you she must have done it good. (*SHE exits.*)

RAVENSWAAL (*Picks up the phone, HE feels the buttons.*) Four. One. One A snap ... Yes. The Deer Park Water Company, please. (*Angry*) In Morocco! New York, where do you think? (*Pause*) Thank you. (*Hangs up, starts to dial again*) Five. Five. Five. Three. Three. Two. Nine ... (*Searches for the nine . finds it. Tentative*) Hello? (*Triumphant*) Yes! I'd like to speak to—(*Thinks.*) the boss, Forrest? ... Forrester, right ... I'm calling about Anita Merendino ... Thank you ... Yes, Mr. Forrester? I'd like to know if Miss Merendino came to work today ... Who am I? I'm a reporter for "60 Minutes." We're doing a story on fellatio in the bottled water business ... Ah! I see I've got your attention now ... Yes? ... Yes .... How badly? ... I see ...

NURSE. (*Enters with empty trash can.*) There was a message for you at the reception desk from your girlfriend.

RAVENSWAAL. (*Quickly into phone*) Thank you. Goodbye. (*Hangs up.*) What's the message?

NURSE Merendino's not coming. She had an accident.

RAVENSWAAL. I just heard that on the phone. Where is she?

NURSE. Anita is *here*. In the hospital. Her boyfriend punched her and knocked her down the stairs. Maybe she broke her shoulder. They don't know. She's in X-ray.

RAVENSWAAL. Can you take me to her? Can I talk to her ... (*HE starts to get up.*)

NURSE. Easy, boy. I can't believe an old guy like you, could get so *aroused* I mean one time she doesn't show up here and you want to go chasing after her. You are awesome.

RAVENSWAAL. I gather that in some odd, perverse way you think you're paying me a compliment, but I am weary of *these vulgar* innuendos. You don't know anything about what I feel or think so please let's return to the comfort of our previous relationship.

NURSE. What relationship?

RAVENSWAAL. Hostile patient, and bitchy nurse.

NURSE. Fine with me. Good-bye.

RAVENSWAAL. Wait! How can I find her?

NURSE. I have other patients! (*NURSE exits shutting door.*)

RAVENSWAAL. Wait!

(*HE's alone Frustrated HE grimaces in pain, then gropes for the phone The bathroom door opens very quietly and DOMINIC DE CAESAR enters. HE's very good looking, excessively virile, about Anita's age HE tiptoes across to RAVENSWAAL, who has dialed the operator)*

RAVENSWAAL. Operator. Connect me to the X-ray department, please. Yes. I'm looking for Anita Merendino. She's there being X-rayed. M-e-r-e—

(DOMINIC has placed his finger on the hang-up button on the phone. RAVENSWAAL feels the phone go dead. HE reaches to click it and feels Dominic's hand DOMINIC, gently, takes the phone from Ravenswaal and hangs it up)

RAVENSWAAL. Raul?

DOMINIC. You Ravenswaal?

RAVENSWAAL. Yes. Are you a new orderly?

DOMINIC. *(Offended)* No. Do I look like—Oh, yeah, that's right, you're blind. *(Leans into him and yells in his ear.)* Hey, that must be a bitch!

RAVENSWAAL. *(Reacts, then quietly.)* Why would you scream at a blind man?

DOMINIC. Yeah that's right, blind *not* deaf. Hey! What was that movie about the blind *and* deaf girl? Ruby Keeler?

(Pause)

RAVENSWAAL. Helen Keller!

DOMINIC. Helen Keller, that's right. I loved her. Helen spit on her teacher. I never forgot that. Guess who I am?

RAVENSWAAL. William F. Buckley.

DOMINIC. *(Confused.)* No. I'm a friend of Anita's.

RAVENSWAAL. Dominic.

DOMINIC Dominic De Caesar.

RAVENSWAAL. Of the New Jersey oil drum De Caesars?

DOMINIC. She told you about that, huh? Well, I'm none other than he. I had to come through your bathroom window—cops are looking for me.

RAVENSWAAL. As well they might.

DOMINIC. Yeah, but they ain't gonna find me. Listen. I owe you. You possibly saved my life with that check. And what I owe, I pay You like watermelon?

RAVENSWAAL. What?

DOMINIC. Watermelon. You like it?

RAVENSWAAL. It's   a pleasant enough fruit.

DOMINIC. It's out of season right now

RAVENSWAAL. Thanks for the tip.

DOMINIC. You're not catching what I'm saying. There's a guy I know in Mexico, he can get it for me. By tomorrow morning I could have a watermelon right here in this room. (*Sotto*) Even though it's out of season. What do you say?

RAVENSWAAL. I say you're a walking cesspool.

DOMINIC. Not an appropriate answer. What was that for?

RAVENSWAAL. That's for a man who punches a woman and throws her down a flight of stairs.

DOMINIC. Oh, that.

RAVENSWAAL. Yes, that. Very much that. What kind of man would do such a thing?

DOMINIC. Hey, it's no big deal.

(The door opens DOMINIC instantly throws himself on the floor and rolls behind the bed ANITA enters, wheeling herself in a wheelchair One arm is in a sling)

ANITA. (*Cheery*) Hi, Mr. Ravenswaal. I heard you were trying to find me. That was sweet of you ...
RAVENSWAAL. Anita? Run, Anita! He's here! Run!
ANITA. Who?
DOMINIC. (*Gets up slowly.*) Hi, baby.
ANITA. Dommy, you found the right window.

(*HE crosses and closes the corridor door behind her DOM and ANITA are a little uncomfortable with each other since the fight But DOM quickly smiles and wins her over during following)*

DOMINIC (*Nice*) You all right, baby?
ANITA. Yeah. Nothing's broken. I got a sprain.
DOMINIC. So you can leave?
ANITA Yeah They just said I have to keep it immobile
DOMINIC. That's okay. As long as the rest of you is mobile.

(*THEY kiss gently, then more passionately THEY're making noises)*

RAVENSWAAL. Are you kissing him?
ANITA. Mmm
RAVENSWAAL. You are kissing the cesspool.
DOMINIC. (*Stops kissing*) Hey, stop that. Just 'cause you're sick don't mean I'm gonna take any shit off you. Watch your mouth. (*To Anita*) It's the second time he called me that I was as pleasant as you please.
RAVENSWAAL. Did you or did you not strike this woman?

DOMINIC. Yeah.

RAVENSWAAL. Cesspool, it is.

DOMINIC. Hey—

ANITA. (*Peacemaker*) Come on. You two are getting off to a bad start. I want you to be friends.

DOMINIC. I'm trying. What the hell else you want me to do?

ANITA. (*To Dominic.*) Let him feel your face.

DOMINIC. What?

ANITA. (*To Ravenswaal*) You're gonna feel his face.

RAVENSWAAL. It's a nightmare, Kafka.

DOMINIC. I don't want no guy feeling my face.

ANITA. Dommy, it helps blind people to know you better. Let him feel how cute you are. Do it for me. Please.

DOMINIC. (*Hesitates.*) All right. (*HE goes to bed. To Ravenswaal.*) Here, go ahead. Feel my face. Have a ball.

RAVENSWAAL. I'll take a rain check, thanks.

DOMINIC. (*Insistent.*) It's for Anita. Feel my face.

(*HE takes Ravenswaal's hand RAVENSWAAL begins to feel his face)*

ANITA. Ah, that's nice.

DOMINIC. (*Screams, and pulls away)* Aah! He poked me in the eye.

RAVENSWAAL. It was an accident.

DOMINIC. Bullshit! you poked me in the eye! (*To Anita.*) Watch this. Now I'm gonna feel *his* face.

ANITA. (*Stopping him)* He didn't mean it. Come on, be sweet.

DOMINIC. (*Still angry)* All right, who gives a crap. (*Then)* I'll be back. I gotta go get my cousin's car.

ANITA. Tell him thank you.

DOMINIC. Tell him thank you—I'm not even telling him I'm taking it

ANITA. Ohh ...

DOMINIC (*Heads for the door. Stops.*) I better stick to that window. (*HE crosses to the bathroom.*)

ANITA. (*Sotto. SHE crosses to Dominic.*) Make up with him before you go.

DOMINIC. (*Sotto.*) Enough of this. He's a pain in the ass.

ANITA. Dommy, if it wasn't for him, you could be dead now. Say something nice.

(*SHE strokes Dom's cheek to persuade him. DOM gives in and goes to the professor. ANITA stands on opposite side of the bed RAVENSWAAL is on the bed in the middle)*

DOMINIC. (*Pause, to Ravenswaal.*) Hey, Professor—

ANITA. Dean.

DOMINIC. (*To Ravenswaal.*) Professor Dean—

ANITA. Dean Ravenswaal.

DOMINIC. You said Peter Ravenswaal.

ANITA. Dean Peter Ravenswaal.

RAVENSWAAL. (*To heaven) Take me now, please*

DOMINIC. (*To Ravenswaal)* Look, Grandpa, I'm leaving So .. whether you're a pain in the ass or not, you did me a favor. So I owe you. You ever need anything, you let me know

RAVENSWAAL. Other than the acquisition of out-of-season fruit, how do you *even* imagine you could be of *service* to me?

DOMINIC. Hey, I help a lot of people. (*To Anita.*) Remember my dentist?

ANITA. (*Sitting back in wheelchair.*) Oh, tiny Doctor Hymen.

DOMINIC. (*Proudly*) I had some root canal, I couldn't pay the bill, so instead, I beat up his brother Mel.

ANITA. He left out the important part. (*T o Ravenswaal.*) His brother Mel was rotten. He stole Doctor Hymen's car to pay off gambling debts.

DOMINIC. (*Straddles a chair by Ravenswaal's bed*) Yeah, you're getting ready to bite the big one. This is a time to balance the books. Anybody you want beat up?

RAVENSWAAL. No thank you.

DOMINIC. Go back to your childhood. I do any age.

ANITA. Dommy, this is very sweet, but I don't think Mr. Ravenswaal is interested ....

RAVENSWAAL Let me understand the nature of this offer. If I so requested you would actually—no questions asked—go down to Tennessee and beat up Bob Devereaux?

DOMINIC. Sure.

ANITA. What did he do to you?

RAVENSWAAL. Nothing much. He just published two years of my research on T. S. Eliot under his name.

ANITA. (*To Dom*) Eliot is a poet.

DOMINIC. (*To Anita*) I'm impressed. Shut up. (*Then to Professor.*) Where is this Devereaux?

RAVENSWAAL He's a professor at Vanderbilt.

DOMINIC. Well if it's on my way to California, I could stop off and pop him one.

RAVENSWAAL. (*Interested*) How would you do that?

DOMINIC. (*Stands, put chair aside.*) Well, each case is different. But usually I like to get a guy around his car. I got brother Mel by his friggin' BMW.

ANITA. (*Beaming.*) This he really knows.

DOMINIC. I did a study on the subject. Best way—the car. A guy getting into his car is in no position to defend himself. He's got his coat, his briefcase, he's fishing for his keys, forget about it, he's meat. Where does this guy park?

RAVENSWAAL. I couldn't say.

DOMINIC. Well, if *we* don't know where the guy parks—second best way—the comfort of his home. I just knock on his door and when he answers, I give him a new face. First, of course, I tell him, "This is from Ravenswaal."

RAVENSWAAL. You *tell* him I sent you?

DOMINIC. Sure. Or else, where's the satisfaction? He's gotta know what he's paying for. Besides, what can he do? And here, here's the beauty part, if he tries to make trouble for you, you were here all the time. Dead, probably.

RAVENSWAAL. Death—the perfect alibi.

DOMINIC. Then I take a polaroid of the guy all beat up so you know I did the job.

RAVENSWAAL. (*Macho.*) Hey Dom, Baby, I can trust you.

DOMINIC. (*Shaking Ravenswaal's hand.*) Heyyyy .....

ANITA. I knew you two would get along.

DOMINIC. Everybody likes me. Look, get your stuff together.

(DOM quietly picks up Ravenswaal's radio-cassette and unplugs it, to take it with him. ANITA just stares at

Dom for a beat. HE catches her "stare" and leaves radio behind.)

DOMINIC. All right. All right. Come on. I'll meet you in the alley, half-hour.

(THEY kiss. SHE grabs his coat pocket and HE pulls her across the room pulling her in her wheelchair.)

ANITA. I love you. I love you.

(HE stops, then silently, DOMINIC urges her to do something. SHE resists HE's insistent. HE pokes her firmly with his finger It hurts a little. Reluctantly, SHE agrees DOMINIC starts for the bathroom)

ANITA. Dominic.
DOMINIC. (*Stops*) What?
ANITA. You're coming back, right?
DOMINIC. (*Matter-of-fact*) Yeah, with the car Take it easy, Dean Peter.

(SHE smiles HE goes out SHE watches him lovingly, then turns to Ravenswaal)

ANITA. What do you think, Mr. Ravenswaal? He's got a lot of potential, you know. If he could just get a break, right?
RAVENSWAAL. (*Weary*) He's ... a jewel. Makes me sorry I never had a son.
ANITA. (*Hurt.*) You know, you can be very mean. All Dom needs is ...

(Pause. RAVENSWAAL begins to grimace in pain HE grabs the base of his skull. ANITA is worried, SHE gets up)

ANITA. No No. I'm sorry. I didn't mean it.

(RAVENSWAAL keeps grimacing.)

ANITA. Does it hurt? I know. I know. (*SHE comforts him*) Should I call the nurse?
RAVENSWAAL. No! Wait! Give me the pill.

(SHE finds the pill in night table drawer and gives it to him with a glass of water HE takes it SHE puts the water back on night table)

RAVENSWAAL. I really wanted to spend these days finding an answer, some comfort. Some sort of illumination—and instead all I think about is you and Dominic and all manner of minutia.
ANITA. You're right. You're right. I'll leave you alone. After I get my stuff, I need your bathroom to sneak down the fire escape, okay? We gotta dodge the hospital bill. My medical plan don't cover getting beat up at home. (*SHE goes into the bathroom. Then returns.*) Oh, boy. I gotta borrow a sheet or something. That's gonna be a tough climb with my arm like this.
RAVENSWAAL. Your arm like what?
ANITA. It's in a sling from when I went down the stairs.
RAVENSWAAL. Right. Why did he hit you?

ANITA. Oh ... no reason.

RAVENSWAAL. He hit you for no reason.

ANITA. No! He wouldn't hit me for no reason. He loves me.

RAVENSWAAL. Well, why then?!

ANITA. Chopsticks.

RAVENSWAAL. Chopsticks! Okay. I'm ready.

(During the following ANITA takes a clean sheet from night table and sits and knots it to climb out the window.)

ANITA. See, I was cleaning out my place, you know, packing up when Dominic saw these chopsticks. Dominic hates Chinese food. He says it's all made from dogs. Anyway, with the chopsticks was a bow with a card that said, "Thanks for the lovely lunch. Love Bobby." That's the nice salesman who likes me. So while I was in the toilet, Dominic read the card. When I came out, he grabbed my hair and threw me down the stairs. He was jealous, you know? It shows he loves me.

RAVENSWAAL. Has he ever before struck you in anger?

ANITA. (*Reluctant.*) Well ... once he had to hit me, 'cause I had a yeast infection. And he didn't know what it was. (*Warming up.*) Oh. And then one time he gave me money to pay off a loan shark and I forgot, so they grabbed Dominic outside Madison Square Garden and poured hot chestnuts down his shirt. That was, I think, the maddest I ever saw him. (*Almost amused*) Boy, did I get a walloping that night.

RAVENSWAAL. (*Smiles*) Ah, memories ...

ANITA. Yeah.

RAVENSWAAL. It *occurs* to me that your relationship with Dominic seems to be based on something other than a mutuality of respect. (*HE winces and grabs his head.*)

ANITA. You need another pain pill? (*SHE gets the pill and water*) Yeah, yeah, sure ... oh. It's the last one. You mean you don't understand why I love Dominic? That's easy.

RAVENSWAAL. Not for me, it isn't.

ANITA. He makes me feel special. When I walk in someplace with him, all the girls are jealous of me. They want *him* and he picked me. It's nice to feel special. You understand?

RAVENSWAAL Everything except why the girls want him.

ANITA. That's 'cause you're not a girl. They want him 'cause he's a real man. He's strong, he's sure of himself. It's scary in the world. Dom's not scared. He's not scared of people richer than him, he's not scared of people smarter than him. He's not scared of my father. When I was moving out to get my own place my father tried to stop me with a knife. Dominic came over to pick me up. My father said, "You're not taking my daughter." Dominic said, and I'll never forget this, he said, "Mister Merendino you don't deserve a daughter." Then he stood in front of me and dared my father to stick the carving knife right in his chest. He just stood there Real still. Then we walked out together. That is a man. Now do you understand?

RAVENSWAAL Everything except why he threw you down the stairs

ANITA. Boy, you keep harping on that stairs thing. You get hold of something, you never let go.

RAVENSWAAL. It's a *big* something. Don't you see, it's something that's ruining the world.

ANITA. (*Amused*) *DOMINIC* is ruining the world? My Dom? He doesn't even vote. (*SHE puts knotted sheet into night table cabinet, then SHE starts to get preoccupied taking her sling off during the following*)

RAVENSWAAL. *Not Dominic.*

ANITA. Then who are you talking about?

RAVENSWAAL. Your Dominic is nothing. But there are big Dominics Smart Dominics, Dominics with suits and ties, Dominics with FAX's and car phones, with private jets. *They* beat you up without ever touching you. They don't *punch* ... They buy, they engulf, they merge. They have Clout, they have Muscle, they have Juice. They've got all the brains and power and leadership in the world, and they've all got Dominic's morality. If it's in your way, hit it. Do you know the only difference? Dominic does it nicer. Really. Because when he hits you, he takes a poloroid and he tells you exactly why he did it. Pow! Here's for plagiarizing Professor Ravenswaal's research. This is great. Because in life we're always getting beat up, and we have to guess what for!

(*HE almost falls over Anita's wheelchair SHE pulls chair out of the way HE continues to babble on without losing a beat*)

ANITA. Lookout!

RAVENSWAAL. But this way we know what for . You're blind because you put your father in a home. Pow! Your wife died of cancer because you once had an affair with a student. Pow! Pow! Pow!

(HE hesitates for a second, grabs his head, rocks back and forth and collapses to the floor. ANITA screams.)

ANITA. (*As SHE runs off.*) Mr. Ravenswaal! Nurse! Doctor!

(SHE returns with the NURSE, who rolls RAVENSWAAL over on to his back The NURSE begins performing CPR
LIGHTS fade to BLACK
BEETHOVEN'S NINTH starts to play)

Scene 2

LIGHTS come up MUSIC fades out It is several hours later RAVENSWAAL is in bed asleep The NURSE [with surgical gloves on] is taking away the IV from his arm ANITA paces outside room and then enters SHE no longer has a sling on, just an ace bandage on her wrist and up her arm to her elbow)

ANITA. Is he all right?
NURSE. I hope so But they don't really know, they're just doctors. He could never wake up. (*SHE begins to unhook the IV And put a band-aid on his arm.*)
ANITA (*A little surprised*) You were pretty good, there, before
NURSE. Where?

ANITA. Before, when you ran in. You got him breathing, you rattled off for his doctor all his ... blood pressure and his pulse and what medicine he's taking ...

NURSE. Are you making fun of me?

ANITA. No! I'm giving a compliment. How is that making fun?

NURSE. Well ... My cousin Bernice is always making fun of me. 'Cause when I started nursing school she went to beautician's school and now she's making a lot of money and her customers love her and I'm getting felt up by married doctors and people are puking on my shoes and I'm treated like a maid and I'm fighting with *him* all day. *I could have been a beautician*

ANITA. You still could.

NURSE. (*Thinks*) No. When people ask me what I do, I really want to say, "I'm a nurse." You know?

ANITA. Yeah.

NURSE. (*Checks watch*) Dammit, I missed my lunch. Now I have to eat from the machine again. Beef jerky and a banana. I'll be back to check on him. I'm a nurse. (*NURSE exits.*)

ANITA. (*Softly*) Dom.

(*DOMINIC comes out of the bathroom HE's unhappy*)

ANITA. I'm sorry

DOMINIC. Sorry? I come sneaking back up here to take you out of this place and start on our wonderful trip together and I almost walk right in the middle of a circus. Doctors, nurses, people screaming—I could've been caught.

ANITA. (*Placating him.*) Okay, it's all calmed down now.

DOMINIC. Did you at least talk to him?

ANITA. I couldn't. He was like all out of his head.

DOMINIC. Then forget it.

ANITA. Okay.

DOMINIC. Let's get out of here before something else happens.

ANITA. (*Sits in chair.*) I'm just gonna wait for him to wake up so we can have a nice goodbye. Then we'll be going.

DOMINIC What did they give you here? Stupid pills? This guy could never wake up. I heard the nurse. That's a trained person. Sometimes they stay like this a hundred years. You're gonna sit here all that time? 'Cause if you are, you're gonna do it alone. In fact, if you're here another two seconds, you're gonna be alone. 'Cause I'm leaving. Now. With or without one Miss Merendino.

ANITA (*Frightened*) Please, Dommy—

DOMINIC. What, "Please, Dommy"? I got no time for "Please, Dommy." People are looking for me.

ANITA. Look, if I just wait for one hour ...

DOMINIC. Watch this hand. (*SHE flinches.*) Don't flinch. Just watch the hand. Watch what it's doing. (*DOMINIC starts to wave goodbye*) It's waving "bye-bye "

ANITA (*Breaking down, SHE stands*) Dommy, no.

DOMINIC. (*Taunting*) Bye-bye.

ANITA. All right, I'll get my stuff. I'll get my things in my room.

DOMINIC. Too late. You pissed me off. I'm going alone. I'll find somebody who don't give me so much trouble.

ANITA. I won't give you no trouble. I swear to God. Please take me. Please, Dommy, **don't leave me behind**. (*SHE's begging.*) I don't want to be alone. I hate being alone. I'll leave right this second. Please.

(*Pause*)

DOMINIC. Go get your stuff.

(*SHE hugs him and runs out of room*)

DOMINIC. I'm a marshmallow. (*DOMINIC is left standing there, not too thrilled HE examines Ravenswaal and makes a face*) Wake up!

(*We see DOM have a thought HE glances around and goes over to the closet, then the night table In closet we see extra pillows HE opens the drawer and starts to rummage around inside DOMINIC has his head down in drawer then half-awake, RAVENSWAAL's hand moves slowly towards noise at night stand, then touches Dominic's head DOMINIC jumps back startled*)

DOMINIC. Oh, hi. Hey, your nose is running. I thought I'd get you a tissue.

RAVENSWAAL (*Weak*) Emily?

DOMINIC. Emily?! No You mean Anita. She'll be here in a second. You want another pillow?

RAVENSWAAL. Thank you. What happened?

DOMINIC. (*Gets pillow.*) You passed out or something. Hey, what's the mystery—you're sick.

RAVENSWAAL. What were you doing?

DOMINIC. Huh? I'm, uh ... looking at your tapes. You got some opera ones, huh?

RAVENSWAAL. Yes. Please don't get them out of order. I—

DOMINIC. Yeah, yeah. You got way too much Mozart and not enough Puccini. (*Closes drawer.*) Where's your "Madame Butterfly"? Where's your "La Boheme"?

RAVENSWAAL. Dominic?!

DOMINIC. That's right It's me, Dominic. Surprised? Tell me an opera, I'll tell you the guy. "Carmen," Bizet. "Barber of Seville," Rossini. "Aida," Verdi. "Rigoletto," Verdi. "La Traviata," *again* Verdi. Man wrote his ass off, huh?

RAVENSWAAL. You listen to opera?

DOMINIC. No. My mother listened to opera. Then she died when I was six and she left me the records so, you know, when I missed her I'd play with the records. I didn't actually *listen* to them. I'd roll them forward ... and make them come back ... (*Pause, then serious*) But, she left me (*Pause suddenly rubs his eyes in a mocking way*) Boo-hoo-hoo. Sob, sob.

RAVENSWAAL. But you don't anymore?

DOMINIC. No, when I was eight my old man broke them over my head

RAVENSWAAL. My God.

DOMINIC. Ah, he had a temper, you know ... but some day I'll get even with him too.

RAVENSWAAL. But you still remember *all* the records?

DOMINIC. Yeah. It stayed in my brain. I couldn't get rid of it.

RAVENSWAAL. But six years old. You must have a very retentive memory. You should've been able to do something with that.

DOMINIC. Do what? Become an opera knower? "Hello my name is Dominic De Caesar. I'm here for the opera knower job."

RAVENSWAAL. I just meant with that kind of memory some teacher could have guided you into something.

DOMINIC. Yeah, they gave a damn, right?

RAVENSWAAL Did you finish high school?

DOMINIC. Yeah, one Friday I stood up and said, "I'm finished." The teacher said, "Good riddance to bad rubbish."

RAVENSWAAL. There was nothing about an education that interested you? Nothing? I mean, I'm a lot like you.

DOMINIC. (*Sarcastically*) Yeah, we're like twins.

RAVENSWAAL. Where do you think I come from? I grew up in a tenement My father was a milkman

DOMINIC. Well—at least he had a job.

RAVENSWAAL The man had a seventh grade education yet he revered knowledge ... Learned people were his heroes. He trusted their brilliance. *Now* there's no trust. You don't trust me to teach and I don't trust you to learn. Somewhere between my father and your father—

DOMINIC. Yeah, yeah. Hey, look, can we discuss something that matters?

RAVENSWAAL. What would that be, Dominic?

DOMINIC. You and Anita got to be pretty good friends, right?

RAVENSWAAL. Yes.

DOMINIC. She's a good girl, right? I mean she's been very nice to you, right?

RAVENSWAAL. (*A little anger.*) She's been very nice to you too.

DOMINIC. Oh, yeah, she's great. I mean she can make me feel like a king. And I'm not all by myself ... Plus, she dresses good, and she's got a rear end that could make a dead man dance.

RAVENSWAAL. Quite a compliment.

DOMINIC. Yeah ... But, boy, then sometimes she just busts my balls. Suddenly, out of the blue, she'll have an *opinion.* She'll want to do something when I don't want to do it. And questions! And the staring!

RAVENSWAAL. Staring?

DOMINIC. Yeah. Lately I catch her staring at me. Not nice staring. Not, "look how handsome he is," staring. Staring like she's thinking.... Like she ain't sure about me.

RAVENSWAAL (*Happy.*) Really? How remarkable!

DOMINIC. It ain't remarkable! Ahh, what the hell I could do worse They're all the same anyway. Am I right?

RAVENSWAAL. No Some are special.

DOMINIC I'm glad you said that. How about putting your money where your mouth is?

RAVENSWAAL. What?

DOMINIC I had an idea, maybe you'd go for it, since you like her so much.

RAVENSWAAL. (*Wary.*) Yes ...

DOMINIC. How much money you got?

RAVENSWAAL. In what sense?

DOMINIC. In the sense of how much money have you got? All of it.

RAVENSWAAL. A few thousand.

DOMINIC. Great. So you got no family, you're ready to go, you like Anita, so we write up a little will and you leave her the whole show. In exchange we can name our first kid after you. Dean Peter De Caesar. What do you say?

RAVENSWAAL. I've made other arrangements. I've left my entire estate, such as it is, to the S. R. C. V.

DOMINIC. (*Puzzled*) What's that spell?

RAVENSWAAL. Nothing. It stands for the Society for the Restoration of Classic Volumes. They search for and restore priceless books.

DOMINIC. Holy shit!

RAVENSWAAL. You disapprove.

DOMINIC. (*Angry*) Come on, what the hell is that? They find a bunch of busted old books and they glue 'em up or something and you're giving them all your money?!

RAVENSWAAL. Yes, I am.

DOMINIC. (*Curses in Italian, then*) Now I heard everything.

(*ANITA enters.*)

ANITA. Dommy? I'm sorry, I had to find my sweatshirt ... (*SHE sees Ravenswaal.*) Mr. Ravenswaal!! You're awake! (*ANITA has a suitcase and wears a bulky sweatshirt*)

DOMINIC. (*To Anita, angry*) Good, let's go.

ANITA. Why don't you bring the car under the window so I can say goodbye.

DOMINIC. Sure! You say goodbye. And get him to tell you what just happened here.

ANITA. What happened?

DOMINIC. I wanted to do something nice for you, but he didn't, your pal Go ahead. Professor, tell her about your stupid, broken, books.

ANITA. What's he talking about, Mr. Ravenswaal?

RAVENSWAAL. He wanted me to leave you all my money. I refused. Okay? It's all out in the open. (*Then*) Can I have another pillow?

(*ANITA gets extra pillow from the closet Author's note Pillows are used to help Ravenswaal sit up straight in bed rather than rely on the mechanical device of bed machinery*)

ANITA. (*Embarrassed.*) Oh, he did that, huh? Listen, you helped us enough. I'm just glad I didn't kill you. You were so mad at me and screaming. I mean I already killed enough people. (*SHE picks up her suitcase*) I gotta get my suitcase and lower it out the window. I'll be right back (*SHE exits into the bathroom. Offstage*) Oh, there's a sunset. *It's beautiful*

RAVENSWAAL I remember.

ANITA. (*Returns and gets her purse, then gets her knotted sheet out of the night table.*) Well, wish me luck.

RAVENSWAAL As soon as you tell me who you killed.

ANITA Oh, that. The children My brothers and sisters.

(*Pause*)

RAVENSWAAL. I don't understand.

ANITA. When I was born it was so hard for my mother to give birth to me that she almost died. I was facing the wrong way or something. And after that she couldn't have any more kids. Can you imagine, an Italian family with one kid. And it's all my fault.

RAVENSWAAL. Nobody would actually blame you for that.

ANITA. Yeah, they do. My aunts, my uncles, my father. They told me all about it when I was seven. They said if it wasn't for me, there'd be more children alive. So they gave me all their names. Anita Maria Sophia Rose Merendino. That's me. (*SHE takes sheet to bathroom, then is ready to leave*) So anything I can do for you before I leave?

RAVENSWAAL. Yes.

ANITA. You want another pain pill?

RAVENSWAAL. No ... I'd like to know what you look like.

(*ANITA smiles then slowly takes his hand and lets him feel her face The tender moment is broken by an offstage CAR HONK*)

ANITA. There's the car.

RAVENSWAAL. (*Suddenly*) Don't go.

ANITA. What?

RAVENSWAAL. Don't go with him.

ANITA. He's my guy Dommy and Anita. Anita and Dommy. We're in love. I know you didn't take a shine to him, but he's right for me Goodbye, Mr. Ravenswaal. I can't tell you how much—*(CAR HONKS harder.)* That's his mad honk. Take care. I'll drop you a postcard. *(SHE goes into the bathroom.)*

RAVENSWAAL. Why do you stare at him?

ANITA. *(Returns.)* I gotta go.

RAVENSWAAL. Why do you stare at him?

ANITA. 'Cause ... he's so handsome. *(Pause.)* I know I told you a lot, but this is very personal.

RAVENSWAAL. Why do you stare at him?

ANITA. *(Difficult.)* Sometimes I look at Dommy and ... I see my father. They're both angry.

RAVENSWAAL. At you?

ANITA. I can't always tell. Like I brought home that poetry book you gave me. Elizabeth Barrett Browning. And I showed it to Dominic and he got mad. He feels like people just write poetry to make him feel stupid. That's why he hits. He hits, when he doesn't understand.

RAVENSWAAL. The history of the world in a sentence.

ANITA. I worry about when we have kids. What will I do if he hits like my father did?

RAVENSWAAL. What did your mother do?

ANITA. She played the radio loud so the neighbors wouldn't hear.

RAVENSWAAL. Did she ever fight back?

ANITA. She said if she didn't fight back, it wouldn't last as long.

RAVENSWAAL. Are you going to do that?

ANITA *(Testily)* I don't know. That's why I stare at him. *(CAR HONK ANITA yells out the window.)* I'm coming. *(Then to Ravenswaal)* Your trouble is you want everything to come out perfect. Some of us have lives that do not make a poem. I'm a survivor. I'll survive.

RAVENSWAAL. Don't tell me about surviving. I was a prisoner-of-war in Korea! We survived. Whatever they did to us, we took it. We endured. But even *there* some of us used to plan an escape. You're *not even* planning to escape. Everything that happens to you, you accept. Your parents, your boss, your boyfriend. I know why you stare at him. Because you know that you can do better! Anita, there is a life that aspires—that does not just *survive*, but seeks. It's a life that belongs to Anita Merendino and not to Maria Sophia Chonchita Pepeta Juanita Velveeta!

ANITA. (*A beat, then, snickers*) You made me Spanish.

RAVENSWAAL. Do you have any *notion* as to what I'm saying?

ANITA. (*Yells*) I have a perfect notion. (*Goes to bathroom window*) But it's too late now. It's gotta be the way it is. I can't. (*Looks out window*) Ah, now you did it, Dommy's climbing back up here.

RAVENSWAAL. (*Goes to get his cane out of night table drawer*) Good. Let him come. I'd like to kill him. And tomorrow we'll all be on the front page of the *New York Post* "Egghead Smashes Deadhead Over Water Company Bimbo."

ANITA I'm gonna call the nurse. (*Confused, SHE scurries across toward door*)

DOMINIC. (*Entering from bathroom*) What is this, "Piss off Dominic Day?" I'm honking my brains out, out there A security guard told me I'm in a hospital zone. I said, "No shit."

ANITA. I'm ready, I'm ready, let's go. (*HE pulls her by her injured arm*) AAh! Dommy!

RAVENSWAAL.   (*Yells.*) Let her go, you stupid animal.

(*DOMINIC stops HE looks very angry HE walks back toward Ravenswaal*)

(*ANITA tries to stop him. HE ignores her*)

ANITA. No, Dommy.

DOMINIC. (*Leans over Ravenswaal.*) I'm stupid? You think I'm stupid? *You're* stupid! You want to know how stupid you are? Anita, tell Professor Dean how stupid he is.

ANITA. Please. Dommy.

DOMINIC. She doesn't just read to anybody. Tell him what you do.

ANITA. I don't want to.

DOMINIC. He called me a stupid animal. Tell him.

(*SHE hesitates HE yells*)

DOMINIC. Tell him!

ANITA. (*Confesses to Ravenswaal*) I try to find old people who are alone ... no relatives ... and I make friends with them .. so they'll give me their money.

DOMINIC Lonely, pathetic, stupid, people who think she really likes them 'cause they're so stupid, they leave her money when they die It was my idea. She never gave a shit about you.

(HE goes, unplugs radio and takes it with him. As HE does this ANITA goes to Ravenswaal.)

ANITA. *(To Ravenswaal.)* It's not all like that. We really needed the three hundred then I *wasn't* gonna ask you for more. That's why he threw me down the steps. And I *still* wouldn't ask you for any more ....
DOMINIC. *(Impatiently)* Let's go! *(HE pulls her by the arm again.)*
ANITA. Oww!
RAVENSWAAL Dominic!
DOMINIC. What?
RAVENSWAAL. All right. I'll give you what you want.
DOMINIC. What do I want?
RAVENSWAAL. My money.
DOMINIC. *(Mean)* Yeah.
RAVENSWAAL. Just don't hurt her anymore.
DOMINIC. *(HE puts radio down on the floor.)* Yeah, yeah ...
RAVENSWAAL. I believe you'll find my checkbook in the bottom of my night stand.

(As DOMINIC crouches down to open the cabinet, the blind RAVENSWAAL raises his cane over his head and brings it down violently trying to hit Dom The cane smashes loudly on the night table, missing Dominic ANITA screams DOMINIC, shocked, stands up)

DOMINIC. That's it, he's dead.

(DOMINIC gets up and takes a step toward Ravenswaal. ANITA jumps on Dominic's back. DOMINIC tries to throw her off, but can't. SHE covers his eyes, and furious, HE careens around, blindly.)

ANITA. Run, Mr. Ravenswaal!
DOMINIC. I'll kill both of you. Get your fingers out of my eyes.
RAVENSWAAL. Where is he?

(Finally DOMINIC throws ANITA off, clears his eyes and goes towards Ravenswaal.)

DOMINIC. *(HE punches Ravenswaal in the stomach.)* You blind fuck!
ANITA. Dom, no, you can't hit an old man. No!

(DOMINIC goes to again hit Ravenswaal. ANITA grabs Ravenswaal's cane and tries to strangle Dominic with it. DOMINIC pushes ANITA away and gets ready to punch her when the door opens. The NURSE enters angrily.)

NURSE. *(Like a parent.)* Hey! What is going on in here?

(ANITA and DOMINIC quickly fake like they're kissing each other.)

DOMINIC. Nothing.
NURSE. Why is he hanging out of bed?
DOMINIC. I don't know. He fell.

NURSE. *And* you're making out? Are you crazy? This is a very sick man. Are you all right, Mr. Ravenswaal. What are you two doing in here?

ANITA. Nothing. Nothing. I'm being discharged. I came to say goodbye.

NURSE. (*To Dominic*) Who are you?

ANITA. My boyfriend.

NURSE. (*Grabs Dom's arm.*) Visiting hours are over.

DOMINIC. Hey, don't touch me. I ain't sick.

NURSE. Well, clean up this room and then I want you both out of here. We had a termination next door.

ANITA. Somebody died?

NURSE. Yes. (*NURSE takes Ravenswaal's hand gently to break him the news*) Mr. Santoni. Now I have to tell his family. Because Dr Wells went to Nantucket. (*SHE exits.*)

DOMINIC. (*To Anita*) Get your stuff. You're lucky she came in. 'Cause when I lose it, I lose it.

(*ANITA exits to bathroom, and returns with her suitcase and purse as DOM bends down to pick up radio*)

ANITA. I don't think I'm gonna go.

(*DOMINIC is surprised HE seems about to hit her, but changes his mind. HE stares at her a moment, deciding how HE wants to deal with this*)

DOMINIC. (*A beat*) Good. (*DOMINIC takes her suitcase from her, opens it and rummages through it HE throws it on the floor, spilling its contents DOMINIC takes her purse, takes all her money, throws the purse down.*) I'll have a better girlfriend than you by tonight.

(*HE exits through bathroom. After a moment, RAVENSWAAL begins to applaud.*)

ANITA. (*Picking up contents from purse.*) Asshole.
RAVENSWAAL. A perfect description. Concise yet vivid.
ANITA. Not him. You. What are you applauding for? Fifteen years of my life just literally went out the window. Wasted. I'm twenty-Goddamn-seven years old and I got no guy. And it's your fault.
RAVENSWAAL. My fault?! Miss Merendino. Let's make a new plan, shall we? I'll promise to stay out of your life, if you stay out of my death. I'll be damned if I'm to be made responsible for the pathetic state of your existence. It's Homeric irony.
ANITA. Oh, fuck you and the horse you rode in on.
RAVENSWAAL. (*Reflecting*) Fuck you, and the horse you rode in on.
ANITA. I'm sorry. I—
RAVENSWAAL. No. It's wonderful. Fuck you—*and* the horse you rode in on. Only nine words, but there's so much going on there.
ANITA. I can't help it. It's scary to be alone.
RAVENSWAAL. You're not alone. You're free.
ANITA. To do what? (*Distaste*) Date?
RAVENSWAAL. Why do you always think of your life in terms of men?
ANITA. Who do you think you're talking to here? One of your college girls? You think I can choose between

becoming a judge or starting my own magazine? I'm just regular. I'm not smart and I'm not talented and I'm not beautiful ... (*Slows down*) I always figured my best shot was to be the woman behind the man. Without the man, I'm just the behind.

RAVENSWAAL. When you start turning phrases like that, *I'm* no match for you. Why don't you run outside, chase Dommy and beg his forgiveness? Chances are, he hasn't picked up another woman yet.

ANITA. I can't.

RAVENSWAAL Where's he going, California? I'll give you money for a plane ticket.

ANITA. I can't.

RAVENSWAAL. Why can't you?

ANITA. I don't know.

RAVENSWAAL. (*Yells*) Why *don't* you know?

ANITA. (*Yells back.*) I don't know. (*Pause.*) For a second there I just got this ... dumb idea. (*Embarrassed*) That I could do better than Dominic.

RAVENSWAAL. (*Says quietly.*) Ave Maria. (*HE gropes for his books.*) You hear that? We got one. Way to go boys. (*Pats the books*) Good game.

ANITA. (*As SHE starts towards the bathroom, SHE stops and knocks some books off his nightstand.*) Sure, those stupid books got me all confused. (*SHE sits on her suitcase sadly lost in her own thoughts.*)

RAVENSWAAL. Confusion is wonderful. Confusion inspires philosophy and art. Certainty only inspires dogma. Throughout history millions have been murdered by people who were certain. Roy Woodruff used to say, "Beware the certain! Cultivate the confused." Oh! Roy was just made head of the Philosophy Department. He invited us to a celebration Saturday night. (*His mind starts to wander—HE gets up.*) Emily, you better get my suit back from the cleaners, or I'll have nothing to wear.

ANITA. What?

RAVENSWAAL. What are you going to wear, darling? Wear the red dress.

ANITA. (*Scared, touches him*) Mr. Ravenswaal, what are you talking about?

RAVENSWAAL. (*Jarred.*) What?

ANITA. Are you all right?

RAVENSWAAL. I'm ... Did I pass out again?

ANITA. No ... I don't think so. You okay?

RAVENSWAAL I'm suddenly so tired.

(HE reaches for chair, SHE guides him to sit down)

ANITA. Yeah, you better rest. I'm still gonna use your window—they'll be looking for me about that hospital bill. I think if I angle it right I can use the dumpster in the alley to help me climb down. (*ANITA stops and looks at him*) Thanks, Mr. Ravenswaal. (*SHE crosses and picks up books off the floor*) Quite a day.

RAVENSWAAL One last question, please.

ANITA. (*Hears that and stops Pause.*) All right. Is that a toupee?

RAVENSWAAL. (*Startled*) What?

ANITA. You said I could have one last question.

RAVENSWAAL No, *I* wanted to ask the question!

ANITA. Oh. Go ahead.

RAVENSWAAL. Why did you think it was a toupee?

ANITA That was *your* question? Funny, we were thinking of the same thing

RAVENSWAAL. (*Laughs, then.*) Did you really have a blind grandmother?

ANITA. Oh. Yeah, I really did. I read to her for ten years and she used to brush my hair while I was ... Anyway, she passed away. And left me some money.

RAVENSWAAL. That's where Dominic got the idea.

ANITA. Yeah. Some idea, huh?

RAVENSWAAL. Yes.

ANITA. (*Silence as SHE stares at him, sadly. HE no longer seems aware of her presence .. gently.*) You know, Mr. Ravenswaal, everybody dies ... so it can't be that bad.

RAVENSWAAL. What the hell does that mean? "Everybody dies, so it can't be that bad?" *I'm* dying. It's a special event. One time only.

ANITA. I just mean it's a natural ... thing.

RAVENSWAAL. (*Getting angry.*) Metaphysics is not your forte. You have no—(*Gives up.*) Forget it. I will lie here and grapple with the fundamental meaning of existence. You'll crawl out the window with your suitcase and land in a dumpster.

ANITA. (*Gets mad.*) "Fundamental meaning of existence" my ass. I'm sorry, I don't believe that's what people worry about when they die. I mean I know I never died, but all this, why are we here, where are we going, what's my purpose, that's not what people think about. They think about their own lives and what's bothering them personally. And I'm tired of you insulting me and I'm seriously considering not coming to your funeral, which will be too bad, 'cause I think I was gonna be the only one there.

RAVENSWAAL. Oh, you think I want a funeral like Ben Weinstein?

ANITA. Who?

RAVENSWAAL. Ben Weinst—

ANITA. (*Interrupts.*) Oh, the popular guy with the big funeral.

RAVENSWAAL. What an absurd event. All of us *parading* out to ... (*Long pause.*) ... Queens ... Was it Queens? (*HE's drifting.*)

ANITA. I dunno.

RAVENSWAAL. It was very cold. They, uh ... what a day! Endless. Believe me, you were lucky you had the flu. You didn't have to go.

ANITA. (*Confused*) Where?

RAVENSWAAL. Ben Weinstein's funeral. I was there all damn morning. What a crowd. Let's face it, Emily, in my life, I may be many things, but I'll never be beloved. *You* know something, Emily? ... Emily?

ANITA. What?

RAVENSWAAL. I don't care how many people come to my funeral ... really. I don't want a lot of hypocrites telling me how wonderful I was. Too easy. I just want your respect and love. And when I get to the end, if you're there to hold my hand and put your arms around me and tell me I've done well .. that's all I'm going to need. (*Pause, then clear-headed.*) Emily is gone. I remember the night she died. She said, "Peter, can you still see me?" I said, "Yes, I can." *That* I had to see ... Emily is dead.

ANITA. I'm here.

RAVENSWAAL. (*Pause.*) Anita?

ANITA. Yeah?

RAVENSWAAL. What are you doing here?

ANITA I was just leaving. (*Pauses.*) And I heard ... you talking about your wife.

RAVENSWAAL. Was I?

ANITA. You must have loved her very much.

RAVENSWAAL. An easy person to love. Emily was charming, which I wasn't. She could make anyone feel comfortable, which I couldn't. She was ... an elegant woman.

ANITA. Soon you'll be with her again. She'll put her arms around you and give you a hug. And you'll be together forever.

RAVENSWAAL. (*Gently.*) Anita ... I'm sorry ... I don't believe that's what happens. She's in the ground and I'll be in the ground. That's what I believe.

ANITA. Why do you believe something that makes you sad? Why don't you believe something that'll make you happy?

RAVENSWAAL. I believe in reality.

ANITA. *I* think you'll see her again.

RAVENSWAAL. Anita, please ... leave.

ANITA. All right. (*Pauses.*) But could I ask one more favor? When I left my parents, things were so bad with my father, that I didn't even say goodbye. Now he's dead. I'm just ... gonna put my arms around *you* to say goodbye. Would that be okay?

(*SHE goes and gives him a very warm hug. Then, HE slowly, puts his arms around her. HE holds her. Finally HE lets go. HE's misty.*)

RAVENSWAAL. He took my radio didn't he?

ANITA. Yes ... You want me to try to borrow one?

RAVENSWAAL. No. Do you have time to read to me once more? (*ANITA nods*) Are you nodding?

ANITA. Yeah. Which book?
RAVENSWAAL. *You* recommend something.

(HE holds his head in pain a second. SHE doesn't see this. Then.)

RAVENSWAAL. Do you know what Beethoven said when he was dying?
ANITA. No ...
RAVENSWAAL. He said ... "In heaven I will hear." *(SHE smiles.)* Of course, by that time, he was probably insane ... but who knows?
ANITA. *(Reads.)* "Let us go then, you and I ...
RAVENSWAAL. Ah, Eliot—good choice, Anita—the end, please.

(ANITA pulls her chair over to bed as HE lies down in bed)

ANITA. *(Reads.)*
No! I am not Prince Hamlet, nor
was meant to be:
Am an attendant Lord, one that will do
To swell a progress, start a scene or two,
Advise the prince; no doubt, an easy tool,
Deferential, glad to be of use,
Politic, cautious, and meticulous;
ANITA and RAVENSWAAL. *(In unison.)*
Full of high sentence, but a bit obtuse; at times, indeed,
   almost ridiculous
Almost, at times. The Fool

(The LIGHTS begin to dim)

I grow old ... I grow old ...
I shall wear the bottoms of my trousers rolled.
Shall I part my hair behind? Do I dare to eat a peach?
I shall wear white flannel trousers, and walk upon the
        beach.
I have heard the mermaids singing,
        ANITA. *(Alone)*
each to each.

*(His voice is silent Her voice weakens as SHE realizes
        SHE's alone)*

        ANITA.
I do not think they will sing to me.

(Stronger again)

I have seen them riding seaward on the waves
Combing the white hair of the waves blown back
When the wind blows the water white and black.

*(SHE recites these last lines from memory without
        reading)*

We have lingered in the chambers of the sea
By sea-girls wreathed with seaweed red and brown
Till human voices wake us, and we drown ...

(Gets up and buttons the collar on his pajamas.)

        Time to bundle up, Mr. Ravenswaal. *(SHE holds his
hand)*

End of Play

COSTUME PLOT

PETER RAVENSWAAL
I, 1
Dark glasses
Bathrobe (silk)
Pajamas (striped)
Slippers
I,2
Same (glasses in nightstand)
I,3
Same (robe on hook, slippers on SL nightstand)
II, 1
Dark glasses
Bathrobe (terrycloth)
Pajamas (white)
Slippers
II, 2
Pajamas
Strike robe and slippers

ANITA MERENDINO
I,1
Spandex tights (purple)
Blouse
Denim jacket
I, 2
Spandex tights (white)
Blouse
I, 3
Miniskirt (red)
High heels

II
Jeans
Baseball shirt or t-shirt
Sling and bandage
Sneakers
II,2
Add bulky sweatshirt (can have a hood)

DOMINIC DE CAESAR
Jeans (black)
T-shirt (black)
Leather jacket
Boots

NURSE
White nurses uniform (with pockets)
White tights
Sweater (with pockets)

PROPERTY PLOT

FURNITURE PROPS:

Hospital bed
2 Night tables (w/drawer and cabinet)
2 Straight-back chairs
T.V. set
Wheelchair
Bedtable
Small table under TV
1 Chair
1 "Best" chair

HAND PROPS.

Pile of books on night table
Radio cassette player on night table
Audio tapes (Beethoven's Ninth Symphony)
Blind cane
Paper bag with books inside: Schopenhauer, Thomas
   Mann, "A Hooker By Choice"
Purse with change from books
Money (for Dominic to steal)
Note
Baudelaire (poems) w/bookmarked excerpts
Small box of tissues
Clipboard w/schedule (Nurse)
Pill
Cup of water
Checkbook (preset in coat pocket in closet)
Pen

Copy of T.S. Elliot's "Alfred Proofrock"
Ace bandage
Stethoscope for nurse
Medical gloves
Oxygen mask optional for Ravenswaal in II,3
Piece of cake, w/whipped cream
Small piece of licorice for "worm" in cake
Small paper plate w/cake (Nurse)
Party hat (Nurse)
Phone
Piece of paper (Nurse)
Empty trashcan (Nurse)
Wheelchair (Anita)
Pill
White sports bottle w/straw
Sling (Anita)
Sheets (2 flat twin)
Hospital IV w/stand
Band-aid (Nurse)
Tissues (in night table drawer)
Suitcase w/clothes inside)
Spare pillows (in closet)
Address book (in purse)
Washcloth and soap
Medical tape
Watch (Nurse)

Suggested Floor Plan
WRONG TURN AT LUNGFISH

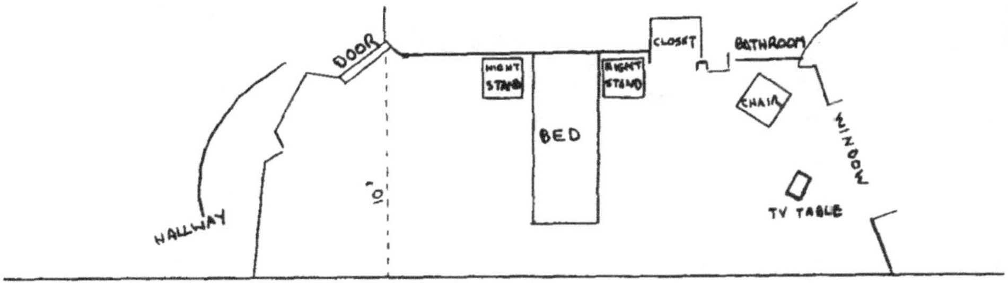

HALLWAY
DOOR
10'
NIGHT STAND
BED
NIGHT STAND
CLOSET
BATHROOM
CHAIR
WINDOW
TV TABLE

(Not drawn to scale)

www.ingramcontent.com/pod-product-compliance
Lightning Source LLC
Chambersburg PA
CBHW070349120726
47909CB00008B/2774